CW00454912

ALEX WAGNER

NEVER BLAME THE GARDENER

A Case for the Master Sleuths

1

"You don't mind if my pets join our session, do you?" my human, Dr. Victoria Adler, said to Sabrina, her newest client. "My dog's name is Athos and the kitten is called Pearl. They aren't trained therapy animals, but I do see them as valuable helpers in my work. Most of my clients find their presence during sessions extremely beneficial."

Sabrina patted my head and gave me a tender look. "Oh yes, I can well imagine that," she said. "I'm fond of Athos in particular. He looks so magnificent, almost like a wolf. And his fur is incredibly fluffy."

The woman possessed taste and style, no question about it. I am a sled dog, not a wolf, but I look very much like my Alaskan ancestors—at least I believe so. Pearl, on the other hand, thinks that there is nothing wolfish about me, and that I rather look like a good-natured house dog. *Cats* ... need I say more?

Sabrina let her hand glide over my shoulders and for the moment seemed to have completely forgotten the problem that had led her to Victoria's therapy room.

Pearl gave me an astonished—maybe even slightly envious—look. Victoria's clients almost always chose *her* as the cuddly animal for their therapy sessions. On those occasions she condescended to perform the role, sometimes with a look of suffering that of course only I noticed, or sometimes willingly when a person came for therapy whom Pearl considered worthy of a cat's attention.

Need I mention what moody animals cats are in general? Pearl was no exception. She only ever did what she fancied, but people adored her anyway. No matter whom we met, there was always talk about how sweet and cute Pearl was, and so on. She should have been a full-grown house cat by now, but she still looked like a kitten. The cause of this was something that people called a rare genetic defect. Victoria, on the other hand—quite the sensitive psychologist—spoke of a genetic peculiarity.

I simply called Pearl the *midget*, for which she occasionally scratched my nose; but that was worth the fun of teasing her a bit. For all the delight she caused people, and the accompanying fool's license she enjoyed, it was important to bring her back down to earth every now and then. That is, to make her understand that *I* was in charge in our house.

Of course, I could have eaten Pearl for dessert when she came at me with her miniature claws, but I was a good-natured dog and I liked the tiny one quite a bit, even though I would never have admitted as much to a fellow dog. Pearl and Victoria were my pack.

The therapy room we were sitting in with Sabrina was brand new, but hardly used. It was located in our beautiful old house, on the shore of a lake in the Austrian Salzkammergut, a picture-book region full of history, mountains, and, well—lakes.

The property had originally belonged to Professor Adler, Victoria's father. In fact, so had I. She had recently inherited both the house and me after her father had passed away.

Victoria had moved her residence and shrink practice here, but had taken few clients in the weeks since the move. She was—as she herself put it—in something of a midlife crisis. Her husband had left her, and she no longer enjoyed her job, either. She could hardly bear to listen to other people's little problems—or even their real tales of woe.

However, Sabrina was an exception. Victoria had immediately agreed to hold a session with her when she'd asked for it—probably because Sabrina was our neighbor, and Victoria had become friendly with her in the weeks since her move to her father's house.

Sabrina was in her mid-twenties, tall, full-figured, as people like to put it, and her hair reminded me of a poodle's fur. It was black, very curly, and cut short. Nevertheless, human men must have found her very attractive, and that was also the reason why she was sitting here in Victoria's therapy room, patting my head: she was torn between two men, and not just in the sense of an insignificant flirt. No, both of them—Leon Kastner and Adrian Seeberg—wanted to marry her, as she had just explained to Victoria.

"My grandfather thinks they're equally great, too," Sabrina said, "and he's a very good judge of character, with a lot of life experience. From the very beginning, he has accepted Leon into the family almost like a grandson, even though he comes from ... well, from a rather humble background. Grandpa is not a bourgeois who attaches importance to money or pedigree; all he cares about is that we all find true happiness."

"Your whole family, you mean?" asked Victoria.

Sabrina nodded eagerly. "Exactly. He really does everything for us."

"And you care very much which of your suitors your grandfather would prefer?"

"Yes, I do," she said hesitantly. "I hope this doesn't come across like I don't have a mind of my own—that I'm still running to Grandpa like a toddler when I have a difficult decision to make."

She laughed suddenly. "Well, maybe I am. But as I said, Grandpa is a smart man. He cares about me, and he allows me to live a carefree life. I can pursue my interests and devote myself to research, instead of having to take a boring day job. I really appreciate that. And I would like to continue to live with my new husband in our family mansion; you could hardly wish for nicer lodgings. So it *is* important that Grandpa and my husband get along splendidly."

Sabrina's smile died. "My grandfather is getting old, you know. He's already over eighty, and although he still seems to be in great shape I have no illusions that I'll have him with me forever. I want to give something back to him for all he's done for me—to be there for him should he ever need care."

Four generations of Sabrina's family lived in the mansion next to us, including various relatives and Balduin

Bruckhausen, her grandfather and the patriarch of the clan. They owned a huge estate, with a park where you could romp around to your heart's content.

In unguarded moments, I loved to squeeze through the hedge that separated our two properties and stretch my legs over there. The mansion was richly decorated with turrets, high arched windows, stucco ornamentation, and with the most diverse stone figures on the facade and on the balustrades.

Some of these style elements looked pretty scary, but my former human, Professor Adler, had been a dedicated historian and had always raved about them. That's why I knew about them in the first place; otherwise I probably would never have really noticed them. Not that I would have you think I'm a dog with a weakness for human architecture; that would be a little strange.

"You can study half a millennium of architecture in this building," the professor had often raved to me. "Over the generations, the Bruckhausens have added elements again and again, expanded the mansion, modernized it ... but still they've preserved the old."

The professor had been in the habit of talking to me as if I were a representative of his own species, and Victoria was now doing the same to Pearl and me. Of course, both two-leggeds had no idea we actually understood them, and they generally had a very hard time grasping our responses. For this reason we seldom bothered to say anything in return.

Pearl believed that it was quite enough for humans to

understand the most important commands in the language of their animals. *Bring me food! Clean my litter box. Throw more wood in the stove so I'll have it nice and warm on the stove bench.* And so on.

In this regard, Victoria did not disappoint us; she was a devoted slave to Pearl, and also met my much more modest demands without fault.

But where was I? Oh yes, Sabrina's love crisis.

"You told me just two or three weeks ago that you wanted to get engaged to Leon," Victoria said, "but now you're not so sure?"

Sabrina twisted the corners of her mouth. "Yes, because now I've gotten to know Adrian better … and I've fallen in love with him. I have no idea how that could have happened." She interrupted the caresses she had been bestowing on me and a dreamy expression settled over her face.

"Tell me about Adrian," Victoria said. "I've only seen him once or twice from a distance, over in the garden at your place. He's a handsome man."

"Oh yes—but then, so is Leon. Both are really eye-catching. Totally great guys, smart, funny … and they both want to marry me. I feel like a fairytale princess."

She bared her modest human teeth into a radiant smile. "But unfortunately, I can't marry both of them." Again she patted my head, this time a little more energetically. I feared I might end up with a concussion.

"That's really a sort of affluenza you have there, my dear," Victoria said. Her voice sounded kind and compassionate, but I could tell she was also overcome with sadness at the words. She didn't let on to her client, of course. Even if Victoria was not enthusiastic over her job at the moment, she was still a professional.

I, on the other hand, knew that Victoria was lonely. Or rather: *we* knew it. Pearl had also noticed that Victoria was longing for a new partner, although Miss Cat was usually fully occupied with her own well-being.

Victoria was in her early forties, small, very slim, and her hair was of the rough-haired dachshund type: short, stubbly, and dark brown. Still, I thought she was good-looking, and it wasn't as if no human male was interested in her, either. The last one she'd dated had unfortunately fallen victim to a crime, though. I'm afraid that had put quite a damper on poor Victoria's enthusiasm.

"How am I supposed to decide?" Sabrina lamented.

I thought now that she'd fiddled enough with my head. I let myself fall onto my belly with a comfortable sigh and stretched my legs. Maybe it was time for a nap.

I still registered a small part of the conversation; for example, that Sabrina had met Adrian at university, where he was studying history, just as she was.

That Sabrina wanted to become a historian was not news to me. She had often spoken about this interest with my previous human, the professor, and she seemed to be an eager and most ambitious student. She was already in the post-doctoral program, to my knowledge the last stage of human study. There she'd met Adrian, who seemed to have fallen head-over-heels in love with her, and had been showering her with sumptuous gifts, along with his full attention, ever since.

"I really don't care about his money," I heard Sabrina say as I was already halfway to dreamland, "even though he has an inestimable amount of it. His family is one of the richest in the country, supposedly. And I have to admit I do love his gifts: pearls, diamonds, the most chic designer clothes, handbags that I would never have indulged in myself...."

"But your family is also very wealthy, Sabrina," Victoria pointed out.

"True—but I would never spoil myself the way Adrian does, you know?"

Victoria nodded. "And Leon? How is he taking the fact that he now has a very serious competitor when it comes to your favors?"

I did not hear Sabrina's reply to this, because at this point I had fallen asleep.

I asked Pearl about it later, but she let me know that she hadn't really followed the two-leggeds' conversation.

"Relationship stuff is not my thing at all," she explained to me, which I already knew. She'd used the time in the therapy room for extensive grooming and had then taken a nap as well.

Barely half an hour after Sabrina had left, the doorbell rang again.

I ran there immediately and was first at the door—and growled. Because even before Victoria had opened it and let our visitor in, his smell had risen to my nostrils through the narrow gap underneath it.

I knew at once who he was: Sinclair McAllister, a despicable scoundrel, if I had my way—but unfortunately a regular guest in our house of late.

2

Sinclair was a bony fellow, still quite young, with chin-length dark hair and a bushy mustache. He wore glasses on his pointed nose that were supposed to make him look more learned. Humans were all too often deceived by such trumpery.

Sinclair was posing as a friend of Professor Adler, Victoria's late father. In truth, he had been his employee, something of a secretary, and the professor had fired him one fine day after I had caught him in a theft.

At first, Sinclair had tried to persuade Victoria to sell him the professor's library and archives, which she had inherited along with the house. But she had refused, and so, with bouquets of flowers, chocolates, and his endlessly slimy grin, he had finally cajoled her into at least letting him look through the professor's book collection. He claimed to be interested in carrying on the professor's scholarly legacy, which Victoria was not qualified to do herself. She was certainly interested in history; however, by training and profession, as I have noted, she was a psychotherapist.

Nevertheless, I could have sworn that Sinclair was no scholar either. He seemed to understand about as much about human history, Professor Adler's field of expertise, as Pearl did about Alaskan wolves.

Good-natured as Victoria was, she'd let Sinclair spend

a few hours in our library almost every day for several weeks now. Fortunately it was located in the atrium of the house, with free access from several sides, so that the rogue could not lock Pearl and me out while he went about his work. Victoria didn't supervise him—she devoted herself to her own occupations in other rooms of the house.

Pearl and I, however, kept a careful eye on Sinclair. We had to be careful because if we got too close he'd kick us with his foot; but fortunately we were both quick and agile enough to avoid the creep's attacks. I'd had to summon all my self-control several times already not to clench my teeth in Sinclair's rear end or chase him out of the house while barking wildly. Victoria had decided that he was allowed to be here, and I complied with her decision. Maybe Pearl was right, and I really was a much too docile house dog.

Even as we'd been watching and monitoring Sinclair, we still hadn't figured out what he was really up to in the library. As I've said, we didn't believe a word about his continuing any of the professor's scientific work, but just what the hell was he looking for?

During his stays in the library he would leaf through all kinds of books, not just the printed ones that were on the shelves and in the glassed-in cabinets, but also and especially the notebooks the professor had left behind. As much as I'd loved the old man, and as much as he must have been an outstanding expert in his field— he hadn't been known for order and structure. The writings, notebooks, loose sheets, letters and other papers he had left behind were a chaotic mess in which Sinclair had a hard time finding his way.

In addition, Sinclair liked to rummage through the professor's desk—he was doing so again today—which was also crammed with papers of all kinds, along with even more notebooks. And he'd tried to persuade Victoria to let him have the professor's laptop as well—but in this regard his requests had fallen on deaf ears.

The device in question was a computer that looked like it had lived through a few historical ages itself, and the professor hadn't used it very often. "Modern technology is really not for an old geezer like me, my dear Athos," he had often explained to me. He had much preferred writing on paper with a fountain pen, researching and thinking, to staring at a screen.

Victoria had already rebuffed Sinclair several times by pointing out that her father had only used the computer sporadically, and therefore there couldn't really be anything professionally relevant on it. And also, she'd stated that some of the professor's private correspondence was stored on the laptop, which she did not want to make available to a stranger. And that was that. For once she'd prevailed against Sinclair's insistent pleading and urging. She had unceremoniously removed the computer from the library—where it had always stood on the professor's desk in earlier times, and Sinclair had grudgingly accepted it.

What exactly he was reading in the books and papers, what information he was studying, we could not tell. Neither Pearl nor I had yet learned to decipher human writing.

So far, at least, Sinclair had done no damage, as far as we could see. He had not destroyed any papers, changed anything in the library, or stolen stuff from the house.

Fortunately he wasn't actually living under our roof. Although several guest rooms were available, Victoria had denied him her hospitality and so he'd taken a room in a small hotel in the village not far from our house. Pearl and I had followed him there on one occasion, but we had not found out more about what he wanted with us on that trip either.

Now Sinclair had once again made himself comfortable in what had once been the professor's desk chair, and was looking through some papers from one of the drawers.

Suddenly he jumped up, ran over to the terrace doors that framed one side of the atrium, and yanked them open. Apparently his intense study of the documents had made him feel hot. If I hadn't known that he was a rogue with sinister intentions, I could have believed that he actually was engaged in intensive research.

A faint breeze came through the open doors, which I sniffed and sucked into my nose. However there was no hope of cooling down; it was only spring, but for about a week it had been as warm outside as on a July day. All the gardens were already in full bloom.

Sinclair returned to his desk and got back to work. He looked frustrated, but apparently he was not yet ready to give up.

"Will you keep an eye on him?" I asked Pearl. "I'm going to take a stroll around the garden. Tim's working over there." I had spotted the Bruckhausens' gardener behind the hedge and wanted to say hello.

Pearl was lying there inertly and merely twitched her ears.

"Will do," she replied, emitting only a barely audible meow. We knew each other so well by now that communication was effortless. We expressed ourselves—like most animals—with a mixture of sounds, scents, facial expressions and gestures, as well as a certain direct exchange of thoughts, which we read off each other's snouts, so to speak. Only with the two-leggeds did one not get far with such conversations, unfortunately.

"I'd take you outside, midget," I added, "but one of us has to hold down the fort here, and in any case your friend the hawk is back over in the corner of the garden."

"Seen him already," Pearl replied, seemingly bored. "And don't call me midget, fatty!"

I let out a growl—but it didn't impress Pearl one bit. I couldn't stand it when someone called me *fatty*.

I am not fat at all, you see, I just have very dense fur. I must mention it here, so that no one gets the wrong picture of me!

To return to Pearl and the hawk: she liked to pretend that the bird of prey didn't bother her, but I knew better. Pearl, who usually stood up to larger animals boldly and confidently—especially when she had me to back her up—feared that hawk.

The bird was a very imposing representative of its species. When he stretched his wings he looked as big as me, and with his sharp hooked beak he could have torn Pearl to pieces in a matter of seconds.

I was convinced that this was not really his plan. On his menu rather were pigeons, blackbirds, crows, and various rodents, which he found in abundance in the gardens, meadows and forests around our lake. But he liked to play a game with Pearl. He had chosen one of the camera posts that lined the front of the Bruckhausen property as his favorite spot.

Like many humans who are very rich—and take themselves very seriously—our neighbors, the Bruckhausens, also attached great importance to security. Therefore this line of cameras monitored the fence that separated the estate from the street, and the hawk, in turn, apparently did not feel any fear of the two-leggeds.

He liked to use the last camera post on the corner bordering our garden as a vantage point, for sunbathing and for the express purpose of getting on Pearl's nerves. Sometimes when she was frolicking in the garden he would swoop down at her out of the blue and chase her across the lawn, stretching out his razor-sharp claws at her, and seem to be having the time of his life.

Pearl was upset by this—she didn't like being reminded of how small and vulnerable she was. In her eyes she was a fearless and indomitable tigress. She was lucky to have me looking out for her, but of course I never received any thanks for it. In her opinion, a doggy bodyguard was beneath the dignity of a cat.

I had already tried to make it clear to the bird of prey that he must leave her alone, but he had not even spared me a glance. It was occasionally so with wild animals: pets represented for them something inferior, creatures they barely bothered with at all. Although the hawk didn't exactly come across as particularly wild and untamed himself, perched as he was on his camera mast in the midst of a human residential area.

As I prepared to stroll out onto the terrace, I saw that Pearl had already closed her eyes again.

"You're supposed to be guarding Sinclair, not snoozing!" I reprimanded her.

"Don't worry." She blinked, stretched, and began her cleaning routine. "Everything's under control. Have fun in the garden."

3

The Bruckhausens' park was huge. Part of it was an artfully manicured garden with flowers, shrubs, and trees from all over the world. It boasted graveled paths, giant trees that were centuries old, and kitschy ornamental fountains. The back section, however, which bordered a wooded area, looked like a jungle. Many generations ago, an ancestor of the Bruckhausens had decided that he wanted a romantic, overgrown wasteland of his very own—apparently it had been fashionable at the time.

At any rate, that is how the professor had explained it to me in one of the conversations he'd loved to have with me. I had already explored this primeval forest quite regularly, and loved it very much. There were hints of human influence in it: ruins that had been artificially created, and which looked like the remains of ancient temples or crumbling mansions, statues made of marble or bronze, a small stream that had once been dug by human hands ... nevertheless, on this fine piece of earth, I felt like a wolf roaming in the wilderness.

But today I was not drawn there; I merely walked up to the hedge that marked the boundary between Victoria's property and that of the Bruckhausens. Directly behind it Tim Mortensen, our neighbors' gardener, was busy planting a flower bed.

I noticed that today he was not, as he so often was, the

only person out in the extensive park. On the contrary, the bright spring weather had apparently lured almost all the mansion's inhabitants outdoors.

On the large terrace, which directly adjoined the house and offered a view down to the lake, sat Amalia, one of old Balduin's daughters and thus Sabrina's aunt. She was surrounded by her three children—her drooling, stinking, noisy little monsters, as Pearl called them. Two of them were still very small: one crawling on all fours, the other already walking, but falling on its nose more often than it covered any real distance.

Marlene, the eldest, was an even bigger thorn in Pearl's side than the hawk that liked to chase her. This little girl, about six or seven years old, was amazingly nimble on her feet, and had a particular crush on the kitten. She always wanted to play with the tiny one, to pet her, to 'do Pearl's hair' with one of her doll brushes, or even to dress her in some doll's clothes.

Need I mention how much that went against Pearl's grain? But even a few violent scratches had not been able to convince Marlene that the midget was not a cuddly toy. She found the little *hissy-tiger*, as she called Pearl, irresistibly cute.

Tiny and I often visited the Bruckhausens' property, as I've said, but we gave Amalia and her children a wide berth whenever possible. Victoria, however, invited them to join us in the garden once, since spring had started acting as if it were summer. They had come for an afternoon snack, and Pearl had been forced to go into hiding to avoid falling into the hands of Marlene, who'd been eager to play.

Closer to our hedge than Amalia and her children, I now discovered more descendants of Balduin Bruckhausen's, also living under his roof: Maxim, the old man's son, Edith, his wife, and Fabius, their offspring. They had settled down on some colorfully-upholstered outdoor sofas in the shade of a huge plane tree.

Pearl and I hardly had anything to do with them; they were unobtrusive people who liked to spend time in the garden, but were neither outright haters of pets nor over-eager animal lovers. Maxim suffered from some chronic illness that weakened him quite a lot, Edith cared for him like a saint, and Fabius ... well, he was what people called a party lion. Even though to my eyes he looked more like a puny hyena than a king of the savannah.

Fabius was in his late twenties, and as far as I could tell from people's conversations he had never worked a day in his life. He hadn't even pursued any studies, but simply indulged himself in pure idleness. So at least in Pearl's opinion he was doing everything right.

My professor had often remarked to me with admiration how generously his friend Balduin Bruckhausen, the *patriarch* as he'd liked to call him, fed and financed the whole of his far-flung clan. "Here we have before us, my dear Athos, a family that still lives in the nineteenth century. Gainful employment is frowned upon, and idleness is elevated to a noble art. Fascinating, isn't it?" And Fabius was a true master of this art.

He and his parents were now being waited upon by

Erwin, the family's valet, who was serving tea and coffee on a silver tray. Besides Marlene, this man was the second inhabitant of the mansion to whom Pearl and I gave a wide berth. He hated Tiny and me with fervor, and probably all animals too from the looks of it. He seemed to loathe Tim, the gardener, as well.

On closer inspection, perhaps everyone except Balduin was repugnant to him. He was fanatically loyal to the old patriarch, however. Erwin was an old man himself, and had been in the family's service for decades, but he was still surprisingly nimble on his feet.

When Pearl and I were guests at the Bruckhausens' mansion with Victoria, roaming the house alone, we had to stay out of Erwin's way. Otherwise we made acquaintance with his broom, got a kick or at the very least reaped a spiteful scolding. In his opinion, animals only made everything 'dirty' and had no place in a civilized household. But he wasn't fond of wild animals either. If he thought himself unobserved, he threw stones even at the graceful swans peacefully gliding on the lake.

My professor had often said that a person's body is the mirror of their soul, and as far as Erwin was concerned this seemed to be true. The man looked as repulsive as his actions were abhorrent. He had a nose reminiscent of a hawk's beak, and from it grew great tufts of dark hair. His teeth were yellow and smelled rotten, his hands resembled paws—only the dark servant's suit he wore was always meticulously clean, ironed and well-groomed.

So much for our neighbors, but actually I had come to say hello to Tim, the Bruckhausens' gardener.

I yelped a joyful greeting to him, pushed my way through the hedge and ran towards him wagging my tail. I liked Tim. He was invariably in a good mood, always had a kind word for Pearl and me and was very patient with us. Even when I broke off a branch in the hedge—which was inevitable when squeezing through—dug a hole in a flower bed in a frenzy of good humor, or played catch with Pearl between Tim's freshly planted saplings, he never got angry with us.

Sometimes, when he wasn't too busy, he would play with me. He'd throw balls, sticks, and occasionally even a Frisbee disc for me. Pearl would never have deigned to chase after any thrown objects; that was strictly beneath her feline dignity. But I enjoyed it.

And, perhaps most importantly when it came to Tim: he was fond of Victoria. And she seemed to like him, too. At any rate, I had seen the two of them chatting and giggling together at the hedge more often in recent weeks, sharing longer conversations than might have been the case from pure politeness.

Tim was, as far as a mere dog could tell, a handsome representative of the human species. He was in his mid-thirties, a few years younger than Victoria, had reddish-blond hair that fell to his shoulders, and these aforesaid shoulders were as muscular as human women liked them to be. In Tim's blue eyes there always seemed to be a friendly smile, which he was ready to bestow on just about anyone.

I decided that Tim and Victoria had to be paired together. If Sabrina's grandpa was concerned about her love life and choosing the best spouse for her, it was only right that I arrange some romantic bliss for Victoria. Of course it was also important that her potential new husband got along with Pearl and me, and she didn't end up falling for a guy like Sinclair McAllister, who made a habit of kicking us when she wasn't looking.

4

Just as I was about to start pondering a possible plan for pairing Tim with Victoria, Father Valentin showed up on his bicycle.

Tim walked to the fence that bordered the sidewalk where the priest had stopped, and I skipped cheerfully along behind.

The priest was also a pleasant two-legged, and I was fond of him. During my professor's lifetime, the two had been close friends. Father Valentin was only a few years younger, had white hair and a nose as indented as that of a bulldog. You usually sniffed him out before you saw him, because he always smelled of the menthol cigarettes that he loved to smoke so passionately.

He looked down at me. "Well, Athos, how have you been?" And turning to Tim, he added, "Such a magnificent animal, isn't he?"

I grew a few inches with pride, and immediately a few more as Tim nodded vigorously in agreement with the priest.

"I think he has taken the death of his master well," said Tim, "and is now in the very best hands with the professor's daughter."

The priest narrowed his eyes, gave Tim a penetrating look, and suddenly smiled. "I must say, Victoria is a real asset, isn't she? Not only to this dog, but also to our community. I just have to get her to drop by the church sometime," he added.

"I'm sure you'll succeed, Father," Tim said. "Uh, I'm not a frequent visitor to your church myself, I must admit, but your sermons are very ... well, impressive. With your descriptions of hellfire, one could easily imagine oneself in a movie theater!"

The priest grinned mischievously. He seemed lost in thought for a moment, then raised his head and looked the young gardener straight in the eye. "You're quite fond—of Victoria, I mean. Not of my sermons. Aren't you?"

"Excuse me?" Tim looked startled. The next moment he'd averted his gaze and begun picking at the branches of the laurel bush next to him. I can't call myself a gardening expert, but to my eye the shrub didn't look the least bit like it needed a gardener's attention.

The priest's grin widened. He leaned his bike against the fence and stepped closer to Tim.

"You really don't have to deny it to me, my son," he said in a kindly voice. "Nothing human is alien to me, as the ancient Romans liked to say. And if you want my rather inconsequential opinion: I think Victoria has taken quite a liking to you, too. I may be an old geezer without any experience with women, but that seems obvious to me."

Tim plucked a few more leaves from the poor shrub which by now was looking the worse for wear.

"Victoria does have that guy in her house," he said. "That Sinclair fellow. Terrible chap, if you ask me, but there's no accounting for taste. Anyway, I don't think I ought to fancy my chances with her."

"Hmm," said the priest. "A very unpleasant fellow, indeed. But I don't think he's after Victoria's *heart*, if that's what you think, my son."

"Isn't he? How do you know what he is up to? Nothing good, anyway, if you ask me!"

"Yeah, I suppose not. And I don't really understand why Victoria lets him near her at all, when her father threw the scoundrel out of the house. The professor didn't express himself very clearly to me at the time, but I think that this McAllister stole something from him. Anyway, Professor Adler was very disappointed in the man."

I interfered in the conversation of my two-legged friends with excited yapping. Events had transpired in exactly the way that the priest assumed. And I'd caught the creep McAllister red-handed in the theft!

The men took no notice of me. Instead, Tim asked Father Valentin, "Does Victoria actually know about this? About his ejection from the house? And that she might be allowing access to a thief?"

"No!" I yelped urgently, "she hasn't the slightest idea. You two have to make it clear to her—warn her, protect her!"

Only then did I remember in my excitement that the two of them couldn't understand me.

I sat down resignedly on my hindquarters and started panting in my frustration. Why was it actually as hot in March as it usually was in July? Was this the so-called climate change of which the two-leggeds always loved to speak? If so then I, as an Alaskan Malamute, should probably get myself removable fur.

Father Valentine raised his eyebrows. "Well, *I* haven't told Victoria about McAllister's dismissal," he said to Tim. "You don't think the professor mentioned it to her back when he kicked him out of the house?"

Tim shrugged his shoulders. "I don't know. Were they very close, then, father and daughter? I hardly ever saw Victoria here at the professor's house."

"Yes, well, that's true ... but he did visit her regularly, as far as I know. At her place."

Father Valentin paused and fiddled with his priestly collar. "As for Mr. McAllister, as little as I think of him personally, I cannot and will not speak ill of the man to Victoria. Doesn't everyone deserve a second chance, in the eyes of our Lord?"

"I don't want to slander the guy either," Tim said quickly. "But I just don't have a good feeling about him. And oh, by the way—that business about the desecrated grave in your cemetery—I'm pretty sure now that he had something to do with it."

"What are you saying?" The priest stretched out his hand and clasped his fingers in the fence, as if he needed to brace himself.

I'd also heard about the desecrated grave. The priest had been talking about nothing else for days. He had probably already lamented sorrowfully about it to the whole village—including Victoria.

Father Valentin was quite stern about this particular

sacrilege. He had already accused me of desecrating tombs once before, simply because I had peed on a grave in the cemetery. The tombstones and the slabs that covered some of the graves were optimal places to leave a scent mark, but unfortunately the two-leggeds didn't know the first thing about the art.

The current grave desecration, however, seemed to have involved a more serious incident. Apparently someone had tried to push the stone slab off one of the graves a few days ago—and had broken it in the process. The grave was one of the most imposing in the cemetery, guarded by a stone angel holding a flaming sword that looked quite lifelike.

According to the priest, the body—the woman whose final resting place was in the grave in question—was still on site and had not suffered any damage. Nevertheless the poor man of God was beside himself over such a heinous violation.

"You know, Tim," the priest was saying, "since we were just talking about Professor Adler … I just remembered that he once addressed me about that very grave. It must have been two or three weeks before he died. He asked me about the young woman who is buried there, Käthe Küpper. But she died a good hundred years ago, so I had to tell him that I knew absolutely nothing about her."

"And why did the professor take an interest in her, then?" Tim asked, looking puzzled.

"Oh, I guess it had to do with his research at the time. He didn't give me a specific reason."

Tim frowned. "Well, maybe McAllister is on the trail of that very research, and that's why he desecrated the grave," he said. "He must have been looking for something in it."

"You really think *he* committed this outrage?"

"Yes. That's what I was about to tell you. But you really mustn't think that I want to badmouth the man ... just because of Victoria," he added hesitantly. "If she prefers him to me, I don't want to be a sore loser!"

"Yes, of course, I would never think that of you, my son," the priest affirmed. "And now go ahead and tell me what you know. I'll definitely press charges against the man when I have proof against him in my hands!"

Tim pinched his lips together. "Well, as for proof...."

The priest, however, was even more eager to know what was going on. "Come on, out with it!" he urged Tim once again, sounding quite brisk for a man of God. "Even though you may not be one hundred percent sure after all—if it is not enough for an indictment, I will be silent as the grave about your report. I promise."

He interrupted himself, frowning: "Well, that's perhaps a poor word choice under the circumstances. But you know what I mean. No one will accuse you of slander, I promise."

Tim nodded. "Well, you showed me the grave, didn't you—the slab that was pushed down and had broken in the process—when I brought you the flowers the day before yesterday."

Tim had the habit of delivering fresh seasonal flowers for the altar several times a week. Whether he was acting on behalf of Balduin Bruckhausen or on his own initiative I didn't know, but it probably did not matter as far as the desecration of the grave was concerned.

The priest nodded impatiently. "Yes, go on."

"When you had already gone back inside the church, I looked at the ground around the grave and I noticed some shoe prints there. They were hardly visible because the earth was very dry, but they were still recognizable if you're used to looking at soil."

He hunched his shoulders as if he were about to apologize. "Police officers look for fingerprints and maybe even DNA traces, but naturally in my profession I first notice what is on the ground. On and in the earth."

"Understandable," said Father Valentin.

"The pattern of the soles ... it looked familiar, I'd seen it before, and more than once. I returned here immediately that day and made sure, in Victoria's front yard."

He pointed toward our house. "The prints left over there by Sinclair McAllister on his visits match those at the grave."

Tim not only brought flowers to the priest at the church, but he also rang Victoria's doorbell and gave her small bouquets from the garden as gifts. On these occasions he had been very reserved, however, and had not said many words, disappearing again quite quickly. But the footprints of his supposed competitor had apparently not escaped him.

As I've already mentioned, it was up to me to lend a helping paw to Tim and Victoria's budding romance, even though I still had no idea how to go about it.

The priest's face turned pale. "This is outrageous. Why didn't you tell me?"

"I am telling you now. You were out somewhere that night; I wanted to go back to your cemetery to photograph the shoe prints. Unfortunately I hadn't taken along my cell phone on my earlier visit so I had no camera, but when I returned in the early evening, it had just started to rain quite heavily. I'm sure you remember the downpour."

"And it washed away the prints that were next to the grave, which were indistinct anyway?" the priest said in a toneless voice.

"That's right," Tim replied with an unhappy face. "So I can't prove anything anymore. McAllister would simply deny everything, and then I'm left looking like a—oh, I don't know—like a jealous guy who just wants to hurt him."

Again Tim glanced over at our house, and I couldn't help getting the impression that he was thinking of Victoria.

The priest was rubbing his chin. "Really strange, the whole matter. Why on earth would someone break open a grave? What could one possibly gain from it? Or was the man acting out of mere destructiveness? And I still wonder what Professor Adler suspected to be in that tomb. Why his interest in it?

"You know, Tim, I haven't told you this yet; I haven't told anyone because I couldn't make any sense of it. But when the professor succumbed to this heart attack a few weeks later, the day before he died to be exact ... he was

34

very upset, you know, really gloomy and distraught. I offered him my support, of course, but he said he had to deal with it on his own, apart from the presence of God."

I didn't hear Tim's answer to the priest, because at that moment Pearl called out to me with an excited meow.

5

I turned, looking back toward our terrace, where Pearl was cautiously poking her nose through the open door and walking out into the garden.

Again she called my name loudly. "Athos, come quickly! Sinclair has stolen a book ... and he's taking off with it right now!"

Damn it, the audacity! We had to stop the villain!

I left Tim and the priest still chatting animatedly, squeezed back through the hedge and ran to Pearl.

"I'll go after him," she suggested. "He's only just left, and on foot. I'll find his trail and follow him—unseen, of course. Then at least we'll know where he's going with the book. And hopefully we can take it back from him."

"You're not going alone," I objected. "It's much too dangerous."

But Pearl pretended to be struck by sudden deafness and scurried off.

We'd already had this discussion many times since Pearl had moved in with us, and it showed once again how illogically humans often tended to behave. Because Pearl was a cat Victoria allowed her to roam freely, to her heart's content, even beyond our property. Our garden fence was no obstacle for the tiny kitten; Pearl could squeeze through the bars without any problem.

Victoria did call out "Be careful, sweetie!" after her almost every time she saw Pearl disappear from the property, but she didn't stop her.

However I did not approve, as I felt responsible not only for the safety of my human, but for my cat as well. I tried to explain my concern to Pearl: "You're so small and defenseless. You're risking your life going off on your own! The hawk could get its claws into you, or a human could possibly kidnap you because they think you're cute for some unfathomable reason."

"What do you mean, for some unfathomable reason?" Pearl worked herself up. "I *am* cute!—and dangerous at the same time. Fearless! I can take care of myself; I don't need a Malamute bodyguard!"

She underlined her assertion with a theatrical snarl. Fortunately, dogs don't experience laughing fits like humans do, otherwise I would hardly have been able to restrain myself in the face of this demonstration of Pearl's ferocity.

As a dog, on the other hand, I was a prisoner of our property, at least officially. I was only allowed to leave it with Victoria, and had to walk on a leash most of the time. "You have plenty of room to let off steam in our garden, Athos," she'd explained to me. "And on the Bruckhausens' property—which is really very kind of them. You have quite the forest at your disposal there, after all."

That was correct in principle, but even that overgrown part of the park to which Victoria had alluded was surrounded by a fence. And the barrier was in excellent condition, so that I could neither leap over it nor dig underneath it.

Therefore, if I wanted to follow Pearl on one of her forays, there was only one way that I could go—and Victoria knew nothing about it. And it was one that required getting my paws wet.

At the farthest end of the Bruckhausens' park, the fence only closed in the solid ground and halted at the shore, so one could avoid the barrier by walking past it in the shallow water of the lake. And from the small wood beyond one had free entrance to the streets, or wherever else one wanted to go.

The path in the opposite direction, that is the border between Victoria's property and her other neighbors, was blocked by some large rocks. There I would have had to swim out into the lake and venture into deep water, just to get around the obstacle. And to be honest— don't tell anybody, please!—I'm not a water lover, nor much of a swimmer.

Because of the size of the Bruckhausens' property, my secret escape path took quite a bit of time, even when I ran at full speed. But I had no other choice; I couldn't let Pearl, who had long since disappeared from my field of vision without heeding my warning calls, pursue Sinclair McAllister, of all people, alone! A scoundrel like him would certainly not have scrupled to wring her neck if he got his grubby paws on her.

So I rushed off, taking the shortest way through the Bruckhausens' park. I splashed into the shallow water in front of the fence at the far end of the overgrown part, and finally reached the road again through the woods behind it, where Sinclair and Pearl had to be. Provided they had not long since taken a few forks in the road and were gone for good.

Fortunately, dogs have an excellent sense of smell! I ran to the entrance gate to our front yard, picked up both Sinclair's and Pearl's scent, and had no trouble following their route.

I found the tiny one in the front yard of the little hotel where Sinclair had rented a room.

"Hello—there you are at last," she greeted me. "It's been ages."

"Very funny," I countered. At the same time, I was relieved that she was unharmed. "Where's Sinclair?"

"He went into the hotel," Pearl said.

"With the book he's stolen?"

"Yes. He hid it in his backpack and walked straight here, without stopping or talking to anyone along the way."

"Crap," I grumbled. "We can't get into the hotel."

"Into the building—we might. We could squeeze through the door along with any of the two-leggeds that go in and out of there. That is, I could do it. You'd stand out."

"That's out of the question. You're not sneaking into that scoundrel's room alone!"

"Alright, fine; I don't plan to anyway. But how do we get the book back?"

"What kind of book was it anyway? Could you tell?"

"One of the professor's notebooks, I think. There was no text on the cover, and it was quite slim."

"Hmm. There must be important things in there, then, or otherwise Sinclair would hardly have stolen it. If only we could tell Victoria that she's been robbed...."

"How?" meowed Pearl. "There's no way."

Unfortunately I had to agree with her in this case.

"Well then," I grumbled reluctantly. "Let's go home ... before anyone notices I've run off."

"Alrighty then."

It was extremely unsatisfactory, but we couldn't think of anything better to do. So we departed, like two defeated heroes.

While we were walking back home, I told Pearl about the conversation I'd overheard between Tim and Father Valentin, and that McAllister was possibly not only a book thief but also a grave robber.

"That doesn't surprise me at all," Pearl said. "Although I can't imagine what you'd want to break open a grave for, unless you were some scavenger who loved decomposed flesh."

When we reached our house Pearl slipped nimbly through the fence, but I had to take the long detour through our neighbors' park again.

When I finally returned home and entered our garden, Victoria had just come out through the terrace doors. Fortunately she did not suspect that I had escaped.

"Well, Athos, did you take a little footbath on this beautiful spring day?" was all she said to me. My wet paws cannot have escaped her notice, and she seemed amused that I am not a really enthusiastic swimmer.

6

The next morning I was dozing peacefully on our terrace when I heard Pearl call for me again.

I immediately got up on my paws. What was going on now? Was she once again being chased by her special friend, the hawk? Or had she been messing with some four-legged predator? She tended sometimes—no, most of the time!—to overestimate herself.

I looked around, sniffed, and listened. There was no trace of the hawk, and I couldn't spot a fox, a marten, a bad-tempered tomcat from the neighborhood, or a similar predator that would be dangerous to a half-portion of a cat like Pearl.

However, I did discover Pearl herself, who was excitedly pacing up and down the lakeshore, meowing at the top of her lungs. Apparently she wanted to alert not just me, but also the two-leggeds.

I dashed across the lawn, and was beside her in a few moments.

"What's the matter, Tiny? People will resent you if you wake them up with a caterwauling like that."

Our neighbors, the Bruckhausens, were notoriously late risers. None of them went out to work, so they often didn't show up in the garden until late morning or even midday, still occasionally wearing their nightgowns.

But, "Look, Athos!" Pearl exclaimed. "There in the lake

... that's Sinclair, isn't it?"

I peered at the surface of the water, which lay smooth as glass and was shimmering in the first light of the day.

By the great wolves of the north, the pipsqueak was right!

Not far from the shore, roughly on the property line between our garden and that of the Bruckhausens—if it had been extended into the lake—there was a person lying in the water, which was still very shallow here. It was Sinclair McAllister, and he was clearly dead.

I sat down on my hindquarters and raised a howl that was guaranteed to get every two-legged in the immediate vicinity out of bed.

The first person to appear was little Marlene, of all people. She didn't understand why I was making such a noise, didn't even look out over the water, but only had eyes for Pearl.

"Drat," the tiny one hissed and quickly disappeared under some nearby bushes.

Fortunately Marlene did not succeed in pursuing her, because at that moment Amalia, her mother, came running down to the water. She was barefoot and wearing only a thin silk robe.

"For God's sake, what's going on out here?" she panted.

I howled one more time and then ran a few steps into the water to direct her attention in the right direction.

It took her only a few moments to realize what she was

looking at, then she probably decided that further human support was needed.

"Father, come quickly!" she yelled, grabbing Marlene rudely by the hand and running back toward the house with the little girl.

An hour later, the neighboring property was teeming with two-leggeds. In the meantime Victoria had also appeared on our side of the hedge, of course. She had left the house via the terrace and was now standing at the small garden gate that led to the neighbors' property, which provided the only access if one was not a Malamute who could squeeze through the hedge in a more direct way.

The gate was pulled open by Sabrina from the other side. She looked distraught, apparently never having seen a dead person in her life.

"What happened to that poor man?" she asked, sobbing, and the next moment she was in Victoria's arms.

Behind her I recognized both Leon and Adrian, her two suitors, or potential husbands, or whatever they might actually be. Both seemed to prefer looking after Sabrina's well-being rather than joining the other mansion residents down by the water and staring at the corpse that lay on the shore.

Tim, Erwin the valet and Balduin Bruckhausen the patriarch had been alerted by my howling, and the gardener had waded out into the water. Well, maybe Amalia had also helped to rouse the mansion's inhabitants, and possibly one of the two-leggeds had even overheard Pearl's excited mewling ... but we don't want to be nit-picking, do we? Anyway, the three men had succeeded in fishing Sinclair McAllister out of the lake.

As I had already suspected, the man was beyond help.

In the meantime his body was lying on the lakeshore, and a local police officer—a certain District Inspector Richard Zimmermann—had shown up with some colleagues. He himself was kneeling beside the dead man, while on the other side squatted Dr. Guido Rauch, our village doctor. Even Father Valentin had appeared. Presumably he had been called for, just like the policemen. His church was too far away for my howling to have attracted him.

The two-leggeds were talking wildly. Many questions were being asked: how had McAllister come to die? Had he suffered an accident? Had he gone swimming or been thrown into the water by someone? Had he gone to his death voluntarily?

From Dr. Rauch's words I could gather that the dead man had a head wound. But it still had to be clarified whether he'd received it when he'd fallen into the lake or whether he'd possibly been attacked.

At first glance no traces of blood were visible on the stones near the water's edge, but if the swell had been a little rougher during the night then waves lapping against the lakeshore could easily have washed away such a telltale clue. Or had the murderer—if there even was one—cleaned up after himself to conceal his murderous act?

"Wouldn't surprise me if someone smacked that scoundrel over the head," Pearl commented. She'd rejoined me after Marlene had left with her mother.

"Quite possibly," I said.

I remembered that Sinclair McAllister was not only a thief, but had also run afoul of the law in the past. He had been charged with receiving stolen property; that is, selling items that had been stolen. As I knew from television, criminals are not squeamish. When they get into a fight, it is easy for someone to lose a tooth, an eye, or an ear. Kneecaps can be broken, and if it goes really badly, there might even be dead bodies. Had Sinclair fallen victim to a violent crony?

Apparently I had been thinking out loud, because Pearl said, "But a stranger, and a criminal at that, would have stood out, here at our lake. Here every two-legged knows the other, doesn't he?"

"That's true," I conceded, "but there are tourists, even if not so many at this time of year. And not every criminal looks the part." Most of them didn't even smell noticeably different from law-abiding two-leggeds.

The police inspector, Richard Zimmermann, now came through the garden gate and onto our own property.

Victoria, alone meanwhile because Sabrina had left with her coterie of potential husbands, offered him a seat and a cool drink on the terrace. He accepted both quite gratefully, pulled out a tiny notepad, and began asking Victoria questions about Sinclair.

"Mr. McAllister has been a frequent guest of yours in

recent weeks, hasn't he? Were you two close friends?"

"What? Oh no. He—" She began to describe to the police officer that Sinclair had been working in the library exclusively, to study the professor's books and writings.

The inspector gave her a skeptical look, but seemed satisfied with the answer.

"When was the last time you saw him alive?" he asked her.

"Yesterday—he was in my library again. He didn't say goodbye when he left, but that wasn't necessarily the custom between us. However, I just happened to see him outside at the garden gate as he was leaving my house, and he left earlier than usual. It must have been around lunchtime."

"Earlier than usual, you say?"

Victoria nodded.

"But you don't know where he was going? Whether he had an appointment, for example?"

"He certainly didn't go swimming off of my property, I'm sure of that," Victoria said. "He did have a swimming accident, didn't he?"

"We have yet to determine that," Inspector Zimmermann said evasively.

The two of them talked some more, and I asked Pearl to pay attention to their conversation, to see if anything else of importance would be mentioned. I, on the other hand, walked back to the hedge and peered over at our neighbors.

I can't say exactly what I expected to get out of it. I could hardly hope to pick up the scent of a two-legged reeking treacherously of guilt for having knocked Sinclair down and drowned him in the lake. And even if I had been able to detect a killer like that, I probably wouldn't have decided to rat him out to the police. It may sound a bit callous, but I wasn't shedding any tears for McAllister.

Still, I wondered if someone had done something to the rogue. I just couldn't imagine that he'd had an accident while bathing in our peaceful lake.

But I saw or smelled nothing on the Bruckhausens' property that would have indicated a crime.

Guido Rauch, our village doctor, was standing with Amalia, Balduin's daughter, a little way apart from the others. He did not touch her, but nevertheless he was bent very close to her and seemed to be talking excitedly. Despite my excellent hearing, the two were too far away for me to understand their words.

What struck me as strange, however, was that the doctor kept looking around during the conversation, especially over at the others who were still lingering down by the water, and he seemed strangely nervous. Was guilt weighing on his conscience?

Somehow it felt like that.

Sabrina had taken a seat on one of the sofas under the large plane tree, and was being besieged there by Leon and Adrian. The two were shooting hostile glances at each other, but that was probably only to be expected. After all, they both wanted to marry Sabrina and could therefore only see the other as an annoying competitor who had to be outdone at all costs.

Balduin, Erwin, and also Fabius, the old man's good-for-nothing grandson, were still down by the water. I was undecided as to what to do next, so I ran back to Pearl and Victoria.

7

In the early evening, Victoria decided to eat dinner outside on the terrace. She had prepared a few sandwiches and poured a glass of red wine, and had carried everything out into the garden on a tray.

But just as she was about to sit down at the table, Tim appeared. He came through the garden gate, waving at Victoria from a distance, and finally stopped in front of her in a somewhat shy posture.

Strange how sometimes even the bravest men seemed to be afraid of the females of their species. As a dog—or even a wolf—one could not allow oneself to behave like that. If you courted a lady dog and came across as clumsy and timid as a puppy, you stood no chance to ever win her attention, let alone her heart. And male cats did not fare any better.

But, well, Victoria seemed to like the gardener's reserved manner very much.

"Am I interrupting something?" he asked. "I wanted to talk to you. About the death of this—*person*—Sinclair McAllister. But if this is an inconvenient time..."

"No, no," Victoria said quickly. "Why don't you sit down? Have you had dinner yet?"

Tim answered in the negative, after a moment's hesitation, and Victoria immediately jumped up and disappeared into the house.

Shortly afterwards she returned with another plate of sandwiches and an extra glass of red wine, then insisted that Tim join her for dinner.

So far, so good, I thought to myself. The two of them were really fond of each other; even a blind man could have seen that. It shouldn't be difficult to turn them into a happy couple. Before my inner eye I could already see a pack that would soon be four-strong—of course with me still in the role of alpha wolf.

However, the topic that Tim had come to talk about was not a very romantic one.

Oh buddy, I murmured to him in my mind, you're really a greenhorn. That's no way to win a lady's heart!

"This McAllister's death," Tim said, "it kind of makes me think. I can't imagine he just drowned while swimming."

The clumsy gardener was lucky; Victoria wasn't repelled by the morbid topic. On the contrary, she even seemed to have had similar thoughts. She didn't look at all surprised, instead nodding in agreement.

Tim then repeated to her the conversation he'd had with Father Valentin the previous day, which I had observed earlier.

"That Sinclair fellow was up to something," he concluded, "something evil, if you ask me. He certainly wasn't merely interested in your father's scientific work."

Again Victoria nodded. "Yes, quite possibly. But I'm rid of him now, aren't I?"

"You won't miss him?"

"That guy? Certainly not."

"I thought you two were friends."

Victoria grinned wryly. "Really, Tim! You can trust me to have better taste than that."

The gardener didn't reply at first, but gave Victoria a strangely penetrating look.

"I've been debating with myself," he said then, in a quieter tone, "about whether I shouldn't have warned you about the guy. After all, your father threw him out for trying to steal from him. I figured no good could come of it if you let him back into your house."

"He stole from my father?" Victoria asked incredulously.

"Didn't you know that? It was your dog who caught him in the act." Tim gave me a friendly look.

"Oh my goodness," Victoria said. "Why didn't you tell me about this before? Surely you could have warned me what kind of a man this Sinclair was! He pretended to be a close friend and a learned colleague of my father's."

"Neither seems correct to me, though of course I can't judge his knowledge of history," Tim replied.

"And you didn't tell me about his expulsion because—?" Victoria probed.

Tim blinked, turning into an awkward puppy once again. "A-as I was saying," he stammered, "I thought you and that man were friends ... or even more than that. I was afraid you'd take my warning to you about him as slander, out of jealousy, you know?"

Victoria's features relaxed, and she softened.

"Jealousy?" she repeated, suddenly sounding like a shy

girl herself. "That would mean..." She did not complete her sentence.

He said nothing either, but nodded as if he wanted to confirm Victoria's unspoken words. *Yes, of course I was jealous. Because I'm fond of you, Victoria.*

Not a word of it came from his lips. Instead, an awkward silence fell between the two humans.

Pearl looked at me whilst thinking out loud: "They're really not good at this, are they? I think we need to create a more romantic mood. More wine? Less light? Some music? That's what humans like, isn't it?"

"I don't suppose we can do anything about the light, or do you want to make the night fall faster?" I smart-mouthed her.

"Very funny," Pearl hissed. "After all, it's already pretty dark, so I don't think that's the problem. A few candles would be good, but it would be pretty darn strange if we went and got those. And as for the background music..."

Without warning, Pearl gave a howl that she probably thought was a romantic chant, but actually sounded like someone was skinning her alive.

I yelped in fright, and the two humans, who had just been prepared to gaze tenderly into each other's eyes, shot up from their chairs.

"Pearl?" Victoria exclaimed anxiously. "What's wrong with you?"

The kitten abruptly fell silent, dropped onto her belly and gave me an annoyed look. "I guess that was a waste of time. What philistines! Don't they appreciate an accomplished aria?"

"Cat music…" I mumbled, trying not to let my amusement show, which earned me an even nastier look from the pipsqueak.

Tim took the opportunity to remember what he had wanted to tell Victoria before the chaos of emotions had turned them both into helpless puppies.

He chose to speak very directly—which caught my human completely off guard. "I'm worried about you, Victoria," he said. "That you might be in danger, too."

"Me?" she repeated incredulously. "Where did you get that idea?"

He hesitated, but then steeled himself. "Your father's death … you know, well, it seemed kind of strange. I thought at the time I was just being paranoid, but Father Valentin mentioned yesterday that he, too, had noticed your father was agitated, if not distraught, before his death. And if there really had been something wrong with his passing—and now his former assistant has been murdered, too, while snooping around in the professor's papers…"

He broke off. "I really don't want you to think I'm a conspiracy theorist. I'm not so fanciful as to immediately smell murder and manslaughter behind every accident … and perhaps it's also wiser to let the dead rest in peace. If a crime has been committed here, or even two of them, it is certainly better if you do not interfere. In case something were to happen to you in the end, too."

"Not interfere? In my father's possible murder? What are you talking about, Tim?"

"I ... I am sorry. I guess I'm a little rattled. I don't know what to make of all this. I also didn't mean to imply that you were just a fearful woman. Quite the contrary; you're very ... resolute and confident."

And experienced as far as murder is concerned, I added to myself. I didn't like what Tim was saying at all. Had we become involved in another murder case, this time in our own house?

"You don't seriously think my father was the victim of a crime, do you?" asked Victoria. "I mean, he had a tragic boating accident—he fell into the water, but he was recovered unharmed—by Balduin Bruckhausen and Sabrina's boyfriend, Leon."

"I know," Tim said. "They took him over to the mansion, put him in bed so he wouldn't get cold, had soup made for him—but then during the night he suddenly succumbed to a heart attack."

"He was just an old man," Victoria said. "I guess the agitation got to him. Dr. Rauch was called as soon as he was found lying there lifeless, but there was nothing he could do for him. Do you think the doctor missed something? That my father ... was murdered? In the Bruckhausens' mansion?"

"No. It sounds crazy, of course. But what was bothering him just before he died? He *was* anxious, both the priest and I myself noticed that—as if he had experienced something terrible.

"Here in his tranquil lake house?" Victoria asked incredulously.

Tim shrugged. "Anyway, he was changed. And what I

also learned yesterday from Father Valentin: your father, just before he died, inquired about the grave of a woman in the cemetery ... the same grave that was desecrated by Sinclair just a few days ago."

"Sinclair vandalized that grave?" asked Victoria. Of course she'd also heard about the sacrilege at the cemetery. As I've said, Father Valentine had lamented his outrage to just about every two-legged in our community.

"It's a long story," Tim said. "I had proof that McAllister was at the grave. There were footprints ... but then, a downpour interfered with them, and as McAllister is dead I guess the priest can't prosecute him anyway. It's in God's hands now, I'd say."

"And you think that my father was interested in this same grave? I didn't know that. I'm afraid I didn't pay much attention to his work at all, to his research ... I should have been there for him more when he was alive. Unfortunately, I was going through a crisis myself at the time. My husband left me—"

She broke off, probably reflecting on the fact that she didn't want to tell Tim about her divorce travails.

A very sensible decision, I thought. Such tales were as detrimental to a budding romance as tales of murder. Or cat songs, at least as far as I was familiar with human mating behavior. But then my knowledge in this area was perhaps a little sketchy, I must admit.

"You mustn't blame yourself," Tim said. "Your father never complained that you neglected him. He was very proud of you ... and loved you with all his heart."

"I loved him too." Victoria sniffled, the corners of her eyes suddenly shimmering with moisture.

Tim took her hand in his. "I really didn't mean to upset you with my words. I'm sorry—"

"No, it's okay. If something happened to my father, I want to know! Go on ... do you have an idea what he was researching before he became interested in that grave?"

Tim seemed to have to think for a moment. Then he said, "Well, in the last few weeks before he died, he was treasure hunting, in a way. I don't know if the grave was connected with that. Your father had made a bet with Balduin Bruckhausen that he'd find the long-lost Bruckhausen family treasure—in order to give it to Sabrina, whom he was very fond of, as a wedding present so to speak."

"Don't the Bruckhausens have enough money already?" asked Victoria.

"Oh yes, of course. But the treasure is probably of historical interest. And I imagine of sentimental value to the family, of course."

"And what is it all about? What is this treasure?"

"I'm sorry; I don't know. Your father didn't tell me any details, and the Bruckhausens themselves don't talk to their gardener about such matters. Ask old Balduin about it if you want to know more. I don't think it's much of a secret."

Victoria fell silent for a while, then asked him, "Do you think Sinclair McAllister might have been after this treasure? Is that why he broke open this grave that my father was also interested in?"

She paused again. My nose did not miss the fact that she had started sweating in the meantime. It was probably not due to Tim's charm, nor the air temperature, because with nightfall it had cooled down noticeably. Apparently the two humans had not noticed that they were now talking to each other in the dark. Only the moon shone down on them—and, alas, it wasn't able to finally put them in a romantic mood.

Victoria leaned over, close to Tim, and said suddenly in a whisper, "Could McAllister have been murdered because of this treasure?"

8

The next morning we had breakfast in the garden. Once again the weather was picture-perfect, the temperature like early summer.

Victoria was finishing a slice of toast with salmon, while Pearl was sitting in the chair next to her and claiming her share of the spoils. Salmon, after all, was not on the menu because Victoria liked it; before Pearl had joined us, my human had always eaten marble cake or jam on toast in the morning. But the midget was an outspoken fish lover, which she had successfully communicated to Victoria, and since then salmon had been a staple of the breakfast menu. Victoria treated herself to the marble cake anyway, of course.

Pearl was a real diva when it came to food. In the beginning Victoria had provided us with dry food, but the pipsqueak had been nagging about it for so long that now fresh food was on the menu more and more often. One day soon Victoria would hire a private cook for Madame Pearl, I'd bet my right paw on it! At least I got fresh meat more often now, too, and of course it tasted better than the dry food. So I couldn't complain.

Salmon, on the other hand, was not my cup of tea— although Pearl tried to convince me that my Alaskan ancestors, of whom I spoke annoyingly often in her opinion, had certainly fed on this type of fish.

Pearl had just scrounged the first piece of salmon from Victoria when Tim appeared on the other side of the hedge. He was armed with an array of gardening tools, but put them down and waved at Victoria first.

She promptly got up, cut a piece of the marble cake she had baked herself, put it on a plate and took it with her as she walked over to the hedge. I sauntered after her.

She handed Tim the plate with a friendly smile. "Good morning, neighbor," she flirted, "would you like a piece of cake?"

Tim reached out and took it, and began to eat the treat while Victoria made small talk.

This is going splendidly, I said to myself. Sharing food with their loved ones was a behavior the two-leggeds had in common with us animals. They only offered delicious treats to those they really liked. So I took Victoria's behavior as a good sign that things were progressing well romantically between her and Tim.

Pearl had stayed behind at the breakfast table. When I looked around for her, I noticed that she had hopped onto the table and was devouring the entire portion of salmon that Victoria had prepared. I was about to yap at her that she was a complete glutton for doing so when the happy chatter between Tim and Victoria suddenly stopped.

I turned back to the two of them—and saw that they were no longer alone. A policeman was approaching them from the direction of the Bruckhausens' mansion: District Inspector Richard Zimmermann.

"Hello, Richie," Tim greeted him amicably. Apparently the two men knew each other well, which was not surprising in a provincial backwater like ours.

The policeman, however, did not smile. He didn't even return the friendly greeting. He only nodded briefly at Victoria, then came to a stop right next to Tim and put his hand on his arm. "I must ask you to accompany me to the station house, Mr. Mortensen," he said stiffly.

"Are you kidding?" Tim snapped. He laughed, probably assuming the policeman was pulling his leg—but the laughter died in his throat.

The inspector did not reply. Instead, he said, "I'm in no mood to joke. Would you please come with me, Tim." He pointed with his hand towards the Bruckhausens' driveway and the main exit of the property. I saw that the inspector's police car was parked in front of the house.

Tim brushed off the policeman's arm with one hand, and with the other gave Victoria back his cake plate, which by now was empty. "Thank you very much," he murmured.

His friendliness toward Richard Zimmermann, on the other hand, was gone in one fell swoop. "What is this nonsense? Do you want to arrest me? Care to tell me what this is all about?"

"We can discuss this at the station, Tim. Please don't cause any trouble."

"Trouble? You barge in here, treat me like a criminal, act all mysterious..."

The policeman heaved a sigh. "The death of Sinclair McAllister," he began, "was no accident. Nor was it suicide. The coroner—"

"Excuse me?" Victoria, still standing by the hedge, interrupted him.

The inspector nodded somberly. "It was murder, Dr. Adler. That has been confirmed beyond a shadow of a doubt. Mr. McAllister was struck down with a club, or something similar, and subsequently drowned in the lake."

"Murder?" cried Tim, "and I'm to be questioned about it? Are you insane? You seriously think I killed that guy?"

I could smell that the inspector was getting angry because Tim was resisting him.

"Until recently, I would never have thought you capable of that," Zimmermann said coldly, then pointed again towards his car. "Can we go now? If you give me any trouble, Tim..."

At that moment, I heard a rattling sound. It was coming from Victoria's breakfast table. I whirled around— and the two-leggeds did the same.

Pearl stood there, right in the middle of the table, next to the emptied plate of salmon. She was coughing and wheezing, shaking violently—

"What's wrong with her?" the inspector cried.

Victoria sprinted towards her immediately. "Quick! We've got to help her. It looks like she can't breathe! Oh God, she's going to suffocate!"

Victoria reached Pearl in a few steps, and the inspector

immediately crossed the garden gate and rushed to the table on our terrace as well. He was very quick on his feet for someone who only had two of them.

Victoria grabbed Pearl's tiny body and tried to pat her on the back, as the humans liked to do to their own kind when someone had gotten something down their windpipe that didn't belong there.

"Call an ambulance," she gasped at the policeman, "I mean, call the vet! We need help!"

The policeman pulled out his cell phone, but seemed undecided for a moment about who to actually call.

I, on the other hand, was fully aware that Pearl was faking. She was a gifted little actress, but in between her gasping and choking to panic the two-leggeds, she murmured to me, "Don't worry, I'm fine. Make sure Tim gets out of here!"

I did as I was told. I turned to the gardener, who was frozen in place on his side of the hedge, and yelped at him with fervor.

That got him going. He glanced over at Victoria, Pearl and the inspector once more, then took to his heels and ran. Within moments he had disappeared into the garden's lush shrubbery.

Pearl went on with her show for a little while longer, until she finally let out one last dramatic gasp, choked out a piece of salmon, and spat it onto the table. Then, seemingly exhausted from her fight for survival, she dropped directly down onto the tabletop.

Victoria and the helpful inspector uttered sounds of relief. "Oh, God, it's over. She's alive!"

Victoria fondled the midget, talking to Pearl in the voice of a three-year-old, asking if she was really okay, while the inspector remembered that he had actually wanted to bring a man in to the station.

Too late—Tim was long gone.

"Was that really smart, helping Tim escape?" I asked Pearl later. The inspector had uttered a few nasty curses, immediately sounded the alarm to the station— and now Tim was a wanted fugitive and suspected murderer.

"By running away he's making himself all the more suspicious," I reproached Pearl. "After all, the inspector didn't even want to arrest him—just question him."

"Interrogate him under urgent suspicion, if you ask me," Pearl said, making it sound as if she were a police officer herself. "Zimmerman thought Tim was guilty; it was written all over his face, wasn't it?"

"Hmm ... yeah, I guess that's what it looked like," I had to admit.

"I'm sure Tim is innocent," Pearl replied. She seemed a little miffed that I hadn't duly appreciated her clever little diversion. "Even though I'm well aware that gardeners are very often the culprits in murder mysteries," she added.

"Excuse me?"

"I'm talking about the TV shows my former human, Fiona, loved to watch. There, the gardener was quite often the murderer, especially in rural areas like ours. In the cities, the murders are more likely to be committed by drug dealers—or by lawyers—and sometimes even by the cops themselves!"

She paused and seemed to have a new thought, which she immediately shared with me.

"Maybe this Inspector Zimmermann is really the culprit..."

"What nonsense!" I interrupted her. "Movies are just made up!"

"All right, d'you think I don't know that? But the two-leggeds make up these stories based on their real lives, don't they? They're not terribly creative, our humans."

I did not discuss it further.

"Anyway, Tim is not a murderer, I know that," Pearl insisted. "And if they were to lock him up, how could he prove his innocence?"

She gave me a reproachful look, as if I were quite slow on the uptake.

"*We* have to help him prove his innocence," she added. "We are good detectives after all, much better than the two-leggeds. We've proved that once before ... and saved Victoria's life. And now we are going to save Tim. He is now one of our humans ... or will be soon anyway. If they don't throw him into prison despite his innocence!"

"I'm positive as well that Tim isn't a murderer," I relented.

Victoria showed up in the library while Pearl and I were having this discussion. She bent down and took the kitten in her arms. "Well, my little one, you seem to be up and about again, huh?"

Pearl purred artfully and put on her usual innocent face, which always came into play when she had done something wrong. That is to say: all the time.

Victoria tickled her under the chin, but then gave her a stern look.

"I wonder," she began, "what really happened there earlier, out on the terrace. Did you really have something stuck in your throat? Did you actually almost choke?"

Pearl played dumb. She continued to purr as if she didn't understand a word of what Victoria was saying.

Our human continued to look skeptical; I wondered if she was beginning to suspect the true nature of her pets, that we were way more clever than she gave us credit for.

But finally she set Pearl back down on the floor. "I think I'm just letting my imagination get the better of me," she said, as if to apologize for the suspicion she had just expressed. "Animals don't put on a show..."

If you only knew, I commented to myself.

Immediately afterwards, she continued, suddenly in a worried tone, "Do you think Tim is really guilty? I mean, he just ran away ... that doesn't reflect very well on him, does it?"

"See, there you go!" I accused Pearl. "She thinks he's a murderer now, too! It wasn't such a brilliant idea to help him escape! What were you thinking?"

"Hey! He didn't *have* to run away," Pearl retorted snottily. "It's not like I made him do it. I just gave him a

66

chance."

"Yeah, okay ... fine."

Victoria stood next to us, looking puzzled. Of course she didn't understand a word, but it probably didn't escape her that Pearl and I were having some kind of argument.

"We have to find him," Pearl said finally. "We should hide him here at our house; I guarantee the police won't look for him here. He can prove his innocence to Victoria ... and get a little closer to her in the process. Two birds with one paw, so to speak. And we'll find out who really murdered this Sinclair guy."

"Sounds like a plan," I replied. "I'll make sure I find Tim, okay?—I'll follow his trail tonight, as soon as it gets dark."

9

After dinner, I waited for Victoria to make herself comfortable with a book on the sofa in the living room. It took her a long time to calm down and actually concentrate on the pages of the book—instead of staring holes in the ceiling or talking to Pearl and me and asking the same questions over and over again. How Tim might be doing right now, where he might be, and whether he really had something to do with McAllister's death.

When she finally delved into the book, I squeezed through the terrace doors, which were ajar, and ran outside.

Pearl wanted to join me. However, I nudged her back with my muzzle.

"You hold down the fort here, okay?" I said—instead of pointing out to her that my search for Tim might be dangerous. I had to concentrate on tracking him down, and I couldn't at the same time ensure Pearl didn't become the victim of some nocturnal predator.

But I also knew that Pearl would not accept arguments concerning her safety. It was better to assign her an important task here in the house.

"I could be gone for a while," I said quickly, "and eventually Victoria will miss me. You'll have to keep her busy, distract her, won't you?" Victoria knew that I often roamed around the wild part of the Bruckhausens' park, but when she called for me she expected me to come trotting promptly into the house. After all, I was a good dog.

"No worries," said the mini-tiger. "I'll watch over Victoria." And then she actually added, "Take care of yourself."

Unbelievable—she was worried about *my* safety? Did she take me for such a wimp?

Anyway, now was not the time to discuss such points of principle. I stole out of the house, pushed my way through the hedge and tried to pick up Tim's trail.

On the one hand, this was easy—after all, Tim worked in the park every day, and so there were dozens of tracks that smelled of him. And at the same time, that was exactly the difficulty: I had to find the freshest scent trail, the last one Tim had left here, which would lead me to him.

It took me quite some time to figure out that Tim had escaped into the overgrown part of the park and had finally exited over the fence there. That meant I had to sneak out via the water again to pursue him further.

In the forest behind the Bruckhausens' park it became easier to sniff out Tim's trail. Here the gardener had left only one fresh track, which led away from the fence and into the forest.

I ran as fast as my paws could carry me. Pearl would be able to keep Victoria busy for a while, but I still couldn't afford to stay away for hours. At least, I had not yet heard a call from my human ordering me back into the house. That was good.

I finally found Tim in an old, long-abandoned forester's lodge where he had taken shelter. He was just about to eat a piece of hard sausage, provisions that he had possibly been able to quickly scrounge up during his escape.

Just three walls of the forester's lodge were still standing, and the roof was only intact over one corner. Where once the fourth wall and the entrance door must have been, there was now a gap through which I could easily reach Tim. He had set up camp in the covered corner, smelling sweaty and depressed, and looking very unhappy.

I greeted him with friendly panting, then barked for him to follow me.

He got to his feet. "Athos? How did you get here? How did you find me?"

He suddenly smiled, even if it was a crooked, tortured smile. He patted me on my head. "Of course. You've got a good nose, haven't you? Good to see you, buddy, but your mistress will miss you!"

I barked louder, pacing back and forth in front of him to let him know that I hadn't stopped by just for petting, and that Victoria would indeed be looking for me soon enough.

At least that gave him a useful thought. "What's the matter, Athos? Is everything all right? Is Victoria doing well?"

He seemed startled in the face of his own question. "Nothing has happened to her, has it?"

I ran towards him, then away from him again and

yelped my heart out. Always this frustrating communication with the two-leggeds...

Finally, he understood that he should follow me. He probably was only doing it out of concern for Victoria, but that didn't matter.

I led him back to the Bruckhausens' property, to the fence between the forest and the overgrown garden, and then down to the lake. When I splashed into the water to go round the fence, he looked at me half in amazement and half amused.

Then he took off his shoes and socks, rolled up his pants and followed me. Back on land, I had to wait for him to get dressed again.

"I didn't kill that guy," he explained to me as we were sneaking through his employers' park, "but how am I supposed to prove it?"

We took a path between trees and bushes, which could not be seen from the mansion, especially not at night. After all, we couldn't risk Tim being discovered.

He was now following me at a fast pace. Apparently he was indeed very worried about Victoria, whom he must have believed to be in danger. Finally I led him through our garden, which was now in complete darkness, to Victoria's living room.

We found my human kneeling on the floor next to Pearl, who appeared to be feigning health problems again.

"There you are at last," the kitten called to me, getting to her paws and snuggling her way between the gardener's legs.

"Tim?" Victoria exclaimed. "Where did you come from?" She looked first at me, then again at the gardener, and finally at Pearl.

"Your dog thought I should come to you," Tim said, and in the next moment he had run up to Victoria and pulled her into his arms. "Are you all right?" he asked her anxiously. "When Athos showed up at my hiding place, I thought—" he faltered, before completing the sentence, "that something might have happened to you."

"And that's why you ran here, to ... save me?" whispered Victoria.

I could see how much she was moved by this notion. Her body emitted a whole cloud of those attractants that have an irresistible effect on human men. She pressed herself up against Tim's chest and hugged him tightly. "I'm all right," she murmured, "I'm all right."

"Good job, Athos," Pearl praised me.

"You too," I returned the compliment. "Although you should start thinking of a new act to distract our human; she won't buy these medical emergencies for very much longer."

Tim broke away from Victoria, suddenly looking a little embarrassed, but at least he didn't completely revert to being an awkward puppy who didn't know how to make Victoria understand his feelings.

"Your dog knows secret ways," he began and had to laugh abruptly.

"And my cat is a drama queen," Victoria added, glancing down at Pearl, who was now indulging in a grooming session with her usual innocent air.

Victoria closed the terrace doors, drew the curtains, and finally said to Tim, "I'm convinced you're innocent. You didn't murder that Sinclair guy. And I think you're safe with me for now—you won't be suspected of hiding here of all places."

"I really don't want to get you in trouble, though," Tim protested half-heartedly.

I could tell that he was only too happy to accept Victoria's hospitality. In any case, it was much more comfortable here with us than in the old ruined forester's lodge in the woods. And he could be close to Victoria.

"I have to prove my innocence to the police," he told her, "although I confess I have no idea how to do that."

She put her hand on his arm. "I really don't understand why they would focus on you, of all people, as a suspect." It wasn't a question, but she looked at him anyway, as if he must have some explanation at hand.

Tim, however, merely shrugged. "I don't know. Anyway, it's a misunderstanding. And I'll have to clear it up!"

"You leave that to me, okay?" Victoria said. "You stay here, in hiding. You mustn't get caught now. After your escape, the police will never believe that you're innocent."

"Victoria wants to investigate?" Pearl murmured to me in amazement. "Is that good or bad? Can she be of use to us as *we* search for the culprit? Or will she put herself in danger and force us to rescue her again?

"We won't let her out of our sight, that way nothing

will happen to her," I said, "but she *can* be of use to us. She can question suspicious two-leggeds, for example, which we can't do on our own. So I think it won't hurt if she wants to go on a murder hunt."

"So where's the best place to start?" asked Pearl. "Who could have bumped off this Sinclair guy? And why?"

"Let's see if we can find the book he stole from our library," I suggested. "Hopefully it's still in his hotel. If we can get it back, Victoria can read it—and maybe understand why what it contains is so important. And we should take a look around Sinclair's hotel anyway. That's where we last saw him, and maybe there'll be a clue as to where he went later on. Or we'll find out who visited him and kidnapped him, and how his body ended up in the lake."

10

Early the next morning I woke Victoria by gently licking her ear. I knew by now that she didn't appreciate such caresses, but it was a surefire way of getting her out of sleep within seconds, and that was purely my goal. I had also brought along my leash and put it down on her bed. Now that she was awake, I stared at her, panting expectantly.

"Yikes, Athos," she greeted me as she ran her hand over her—admittedly rather well-moistened—ear.

She sat up, swung her legs out of bed and discovered the leash I had put out for her. It was a custom-made one with two collars: a big one for me and a small one for the midget.

Of course humans don't usually walk cats on a leash, but Pearl and I had trained our two-legged differently. Pearl insisted on being taken along when Victoria walked me, and so our human had had this double harness made especially for the tiny one and me.

When we strolled through the village like this—me, the imposing almost-wolf, and Pearl, the half-portion of cat—we certainly made a unique picture. In any case, the two-leggeds we met always turned around to look at us, and uttered sounds of delight that were directed at Pearl. I was already used to this lack of appreciation for *my* merits.

Pearl, still looking rather sleepy, appeared next to me.

"Salmon?" she meowed at our human, which Victoria seemed to understand somehow.

Anyway, she rubbed her eyes and said, "You want to go out already, Athos? What time is it anyway? I think we should have breakfast first, okay?"

So Pearl got her salmon, and I got dry food. Life really isn't fair. "I have to buy meat for you again, Athos," Victoria said apologetically.

After breakfast, she finally put Pearl and me in our joint harness, and as soon as we reached the street, I pulled her in the right direction: to Sinclair's hotel. After all, since we had been living together for a while, we had educated Victoria to the point that she usually went where we wanted her to go. Not always, but more and more often.

When we arrived in front of Sinclair's hotel, I gave up pulling on the leash. Pearl pointedly settled down on the sidewalk and meowed at our human.

Victoria was a little slow on the uptake this morning. She looked up at the facade of the house, which must have been from the nineteenth century. "But this is ... *The Golden Swan*? This is where Sinclair was staying, isn't it?"

She had never visited him here, of course, but he had mentioned a few times that he'd been staying at The Golden Swan.

Pearl meowed at her once more. "Come on, let's go inside! We have to search for that stolen notebook. And find out if Sinclair's killer ambushed him here."

Of course, Victoria didn't understand a word as usual, but she seemed to come to the same conclusion on her own.

"Just while we're here," she mused to herself, "I guess I should look around inside. Maybe we'll learn a little more about this Sinclair guy—why someone would want him dead, for instance."

She gave me a brooding glance. "Surely it can't be a coincidence that you've led me here, of all places, Athos?"

"Of course not," I replied.

I pulled on the leash. "Shall we go inside?"

Pearl gave me a longsuffering look. "Why do the two-leggeds always think we're so stupid, anyway?" she complained. "*Coincidence*? Pah! And Victoria, of all people! She really should know better by now."

"Know what? That you're not just a salmon-annihilation machine, but a snoop in fluffy fur?"

Pearl's eyes reflected her amusement. "Exactly!"

The receptionist at The Golden Swan reacted the same way as virtually every other human who saw Pearl and me in our double harness for the first time. "Oh my gosh, they're so *cuuute*! That kitty!"

Pearl emitted a hiss that the woman interpreted as a 'delightful purr.'

Then she recognized me. She adjusted the glasses she was wearing on her nose and eyed Victoria blatantly. "Your dog—that's Athos, isn't it? Our dear departed professor's pet. Then you must be ... his daughter?"

Victoria nodded and shook the woman's hand. "Victoria Adler," she introduced herself. "You knew my father?"

"Sure did: he was a regular guest with us. Well, not in the hotel, but in our restaurant. He ate with us very often, was always very kind, used to give generous tips to the waiters..."

She rounded the reception desk, came over to me and cuddled my head. "And Athos always accompanied him, didn't he?"

I panted approvingly—it was oppressively hot in here—and licked the woman's hand.

Victoria got to talking about Sinclair McAllister without much ado. She truthfully explained to the receptionist that he had sifted through the library and the professor's research papers at our house, and then asked if she could see his room. "Um, it hasn't been cleared out by the police yet, I hope? Or by Sinclair's relatives?"

"I don't know anything about relatives," said the receptionist, "but the police were here ... and sealed the room. Supposedly it will be unsealed today or tomorrow so we can re-rent it. I assume the police will take Mr. McAllister's personal belongings. His luggage—"

"*Sealed*," Victoria repeated with a discouraged expression.

This was not good at all. It probably meant that the receptionist, as friendly as she was behaving towards us, was not allowed to give us access to the room.

I stuck out my tongue to perhaps change her mind in

78

our favor with another devoted hand-licking, but she actually withdrew her hand from me with an amazingly quick reflex.

"Another unworthy one who knows nothing about tender gestures," I complained to Pearl.

The tiny one didn't answer me, but I thought I could read something in her thoughts that sounded like "Your kisses *are* pretty wet, you know."

I dropped the subject.

Victoria surprised me in that she started asking the receptionist specific questions, almost like a police officer. "Can you tell me if Mr. McAllister was here at the hotel the afternoon and evening before he was murdered?" she inquired.

The receptionist's smile died. "Why do you want to know that? Were you close friends with Mr. McAllister, then, that his death concerns you so?"

"No—certainly not. I can't say I liked him very much," Victoria replied with disarming honesty.

The woman's smile returned. "An unpleasant fellow, wasn't he?" she eagerly agreed with Victoria. "And I was beginning to think that you and he ... well, you know. None of my business, of course," she added quickly.

"Do people actually always say that when they're particularly curious about something?" Pearl commented. "Or are indulging in gossip with complete gusto? None of my *business* ... my ass."

"Looks like it," I replied.

"It's possible that McAllister's and my father's deaths are related," Victoria told the receptionist. "That's why

I want to find out who took Sinclair's life, and for what reason." She didn't mention a word about Tim being suspected of murder and how she wanted to clear him.

"Your father?" the receptionist repeated, her cheeks suddenly shining feverishly. "You're not suggesting he was murdered too, are you? Our poor dear professor!"

"Probably not," Victoria said quickly. "But I want to find out, you know?"

"Yes—yes, of course! So, what did you want to know? Whether Mr. McAllister was here at the hotel in the hours before he died? The answer is yes. He came back in the early afternoon. He was with you in the morning, I suppose? As he was most days? He mentioned it to me once ... that he was going through the professor's estate. That was why he was staying with us."

Victoria nodded in agreement.

The receptionist continued, "Throughout the afternoon, he stayed in his room, ordered drinks several times and also a meal from room service. And then in the evening he went out—it must have been around six or seven o'clock. Unfortunately I don't remember when exactly."

Her eyes suddenly widened, as if something important had just occurred to her.

She had been sweating profusely ever since she'd begun her report regarding Sinclair's last hours. I couldn't have missed it, but it didn't necessarily mean that she was afraid or trying to hide something from Victoria. I rather guessed that she liked the role of the important witness very much, and that she was simply sweating from joyful excitement.

Well, anyway. She lowered her voice to a whisper and continued, "You know, when he left that night ... he had a gun on him!"

"Did he now?" Victoria exclaimed.

"Well, there was this telltale bulge under his jacket when he left the hotel. I notice things like that, you know, because I had a fling with a security guy once. So I know how a gun in a shoulder holster shows up—under a light jacket, anyway. I'm sure Mr. McAllister was wearing something like that."

"Wow, and what did the police say about that?"

"The police? I didn't tell them. And you can't rat me out now, okay? I'll deny I saw anything. I don't want to risk my neck!"

"Risk your neck?" Victoria repeated with a puzzled expression. "What makes you think that?"

"Well, listen—when a guy like that gets bumped off, you live dangerously as a witness—you must be aware of that. And when you're walking around asking questions about his death, you possibly do as well!" she added in an even softer whisper. She looked around the completely empty lobby of the hotel, as if she were expecting half a dozen Mafiosi to come storming through the revolving door at any moment.

"Supposedly it was about drugs," she continued. "That's what one of the police officers who came here said in passing. So maybe McAllister went out that night to buy drugs..."

"And he took a gun with him to do it?" Victoria asked

incredulously.

"Yes, but what do I know? Maybe he was a dealer, and not only a user. Perhaps he expected a difficult negotiation? I really don't know anything about this business!" she affirmed.

Victoria let the subject drop. "You mentioned earlier that Mr. McAllister called room service several times that afternoon," she said, striking out in a new direction. "Is the staff member who waited on him here today?"

"That was Bianca, she was on duty," came back like a pistol shot.

The next moment, the receptionist picked up the phone. "She's here today, too," she said to Victoria, while waiting for the call to be answered.

Bianca turned out to be a fortyish Polish woman who smelled of chamomile tea. We didn't have to wait more than three minutes before she showed up at the reception desk.

After the receptionist briefly told her what Victoria was after, Bianca was immediately ready to answer her questions. The two of them settled down on one of the sofas in the lobby. The receptionist, on the other hand, had some work to take care of in the form of a newly arrived guest who wanted to be checked in.

"Yes, I served Mr. McAllister a total of three times that afternoon before he died," Bianca confirmed at the very beginning of the conversation. "We don't have minibars in the rooms, you know. The boss is big on personal service, so people call us quite often when they're hungry or thirsty."

"I understand," Victoria said. She spoke in her calm, confidence-inspiring therapist voice, which apparently also served her well when questioning witnesses. Bianca was talking herself into smelly excitement, the way the receptionist had done before her.

"Were you perhaps able to see what Mr. McAllister was busy doing when you came to his room?" Victoria continued.

The woman shrugged her shoulders. "He didn't do anything special—nothing criminal, if that's what you mean. He was just reading a book, in a very focused way, it seemed to me. And he kept at it all afternoon. Every time I came in he was still sitting in the same place, in the fauteuil by the window. He always just had me put my tray down quickly, didn't tip me, and sent me right off."

"How rude," Victoria said.

"Oh, yes. But that's just the way some guests are."

"Were you able to see what kind of book it was?" Victoria asked her then.

"Not a novel or anything. Something handwritten, maybe a diary of some sort. I just happened to notice that, of course," she added. "I really wasn't spying."

"I certainly didn't mean to imply that," Victoria replied quickly.

Bianca nodded with satisfaction. "Looked like a man's handwriting in the book—really spidery, all but illegible at first glance. Perhaps that of Mr. McAllister himself? But who reads their own diaries with such excitement, I say."

"And the book itself—what did it look like?" Victoria asked, apparently having a hard time containing her own curiosity. By now she, too, was exuding a scent reminiscent of a predator on the prowl.

"Hmm; the cover was gray-blue, A5 size ... the paper was unlined and the ink was black," Bianca said.

"You're really very observant, Bianca," Victoria praised the hotel employee, and she accepted the compliment with a satisfied smile.

"One of the professor's notebooks," I said excitedly to Pearl, "just as we suspected." The little books in which my previous human had so often jotted down his thoughts looked exactly as Bianca had described.

"Told you so," Pearl agreed.

"Do you know if the police took the book with them?" Victoria asked.

Bianca seemed to have to ponder for a moment.

"I think Mr. McAllister himself took it," she said eventually, "when he went out that evening. I went back to his room at around eight o'clock to pick up the dirty dishes, you know. And there was no book lying around anywhere."

"Could he have put it in a drawer?" Victoria suggested.

"What? Oh, yes, that might be possible."

It sounded to me like Bianca had actively looked around for the notebook, but had not found it anywhere in the room. She was a curious person, that much was obvious, and the diaries of other humans had a very attractive effect on most people; if you could poke your nose into someone else's thoughts and secrets you didn't pass up the opportunity, it seemed. Surely Bianca had wanted to know what kind of diary the hotel guest had been reading with such excitement all afternoon, but had not found it.

So Sinclair probably really had taken the book with him, instead of leaving it in some drawer.

11

On the way home Victoria did some extensive grocery shopping, and seemed to be rather more selective than usual. After all she now had a secret guest to feed—and as I have already noted, I thought it was a good sign that she was so concerned about the gardener's physical well-being.

In the afternoon she relayed to Tim what she had learned at the hotel, and they both concluded that Sinclair's murder might have something to do with the professor's stolen notebook and thus with his work.

"We should take a look at Father's library ourselves," Victoria suggested. "Go through his papers and notes. It will be quite a lot of work, but we might find something that could give us a clue to the real murderer."

Tim agreed, even though he noted that he knew how to handle flowers and leaves better than papers and books. Nevertheless, he immediately set to work with vigor, and Victoria pulled out her father's old laptop.

"I'll start with the data on the computer," she said. "Father was so chaotic; he always recorded his ideas everywhere—on loose pieces of paper when nothing else was at hand, in his notebooks when he was working in his library or on the road, and sometimes on his laptop. Not very often, I think, because he didn't like the computer that much. But I'll definitely look to see if I can find anything. It's something that Sinclair didn't get to see, because I wouldn't let him touch the laptop. If we're lucky there's an overlap between the files on the laptop and Dad's handwritten notes."

"And how are we to know what exactly Sinclair's quest was in aid of?" Tim asked, as he looked around the library and got his first inkling of the daunting task ahead of them. A person could certainly spend a couple of years in the atrium that had served as Professor Adler's library, archive and study without reading the same line twice.

Victoria shrugged. "We can only hope that something will catch our eye—maybe something to do with that treasure of the Bruckhausens that Father was looking for in the last weeks of his life. I could well imagine that Sinclair was after it; hidden treasures, the prospect of fabulous wealth ... such things certainly attract people like him magically. And possibly the people who murdered him, too? Oh, and maybe we'll find Father's notes about that grave at the cemetery that he broke open, where you spotted Sinclair's footprints, which my father was also interested in."

Whilst the two of them were pursuing their search they came together again and again, exchanging information about their finds, sipping coffee, and casting furtive glances at each other that had nothing to do with their search. Occasionally they touched as if by chance, brushed each other's arms, and put their hands on the other's shoulder, apparently to draw attention to something. At the same time, they both gave off a scent that told me they were courting each other.

Very good, I thought to myself. My matchmaking project was going like clockwork. Now we just had to rule out Tim as a possible murderer in the eyes of the police.

It was already dark when the two humans finally took a break. Over dinner, which to Pearl's great delight consisted of grilled fish, Victoria and Tim shared the spoils of their labor. Both smelled a little dusty from digging through mountains of paper like two moles, and looked exhausted.

On the professor's laptop Victoria had found all sorts of correspondence, conducted with universities, other historians, book authors ... and with Balduin Bruckhausen, our neighbor. Professor Adler had been discussing the treasure hunt with him, probably in person most of the time, but occasionally via e-mail.

"But nothing about it seems striking to me," Victoria told Tim, "or so explosive that you'd kill for it. As things stand, Dad hadn't discovered anything concrete that could have led to the treasure—at least, not judging by the notes on his laptop."

Tim furrowed his brow. "His latest findings may have been in the notebook Sinclair stole."

"I'm afraid that's true," Victoria said. "And you? Haven't you discovered anything that might point to the hiding place of this treasure either?"

"No, I'm afraid not. It looks like your father had unraveled the entire history of the Bruckhausen family, sparing no effort. He read old chronicles, sifted through records from the municipal library, visited other archives, did online research ... but he hadn't reached the end of his efforts before he died, I'd say."

"Or before he was murdered," Victoria said somberly. "Although I still think he simply suffered a heart attack."

"Yes, that's quite possible," Tim said. "And I *did* find something interesting after all."

He opened a notebook that he had brought to the table. It looked exactly like the one Bianca had described to us at the hotel: small format, blue-gray cover, black ink and scrawled letters. I couldn't read human writing, of course, but this really looked as messy as if a spider had wandered across the paper with ink on its legs.

Tim tapped his finger on the open pages. "Your father wrote a name several times in this book, which is probably related to Artur Bruckhausen. That's Balduin's father, who hid the treasure back in World War II."

"What kind of name?"

"Hathor," Tim said. "It was probably the pet name of the woman—Käthe Küpper—whose grave Sinclair desecrated in our cemetery. Was she perhaps a mistress of Artur's? I'm not sure."

"Hathor," Victoria murmured. "And what about her?"

"Your father noted several times that Artur called her his *greatest treasure,* and that seemed significant to him. To me, too, by the way. Maybe the treasure wasn't about money in the end, but about a woman? And the crazy thing is—it seems to me that I know that name— Hathor. I must have heard or seen it somewhere before.

I just can't for the life of me remember where. Or when."

Victoria furrowed her brow. "This is just getting weirder and weirder," she said.

After dinner, the two continued their research for quite a while, but found no other clues that seemed significant.

Finally, they went to sleep—separately. Tim disappeared into the guest room, Victoria into her own bedchamber. As a farewell, they pressed a shy goodnight kiss on each other's cheek, but at least it was a start. And we didn't have to rush into anything.

"Victoria isn't doing too badly," Pearl said after the humans had disappeared. "As our assistant sleuth, I mean. She was asking good questions at the hotel ... and she's doing the reading for us, too, even if she hasn't found anything too useful yet. It's a good thing we have her, in case we have to solve more murder cases in the future."

"You don't think this is going to become a habit now, do you? " I asked anxiously. "That we're going to constantly be involved in some kind of murder?" After all, Sinclair McAllister wasn't the first dead person we'd encountered since Victoria had become our human.

"Who knows," said Pearl. "It's fun, though, isn't it? Even more so when the victim is a person like Sinclair."

"But possibly my former human, the professor, was also killed," I objected. "I don't find that the least bit amusing! And Tim is a murder suspect. If the police find him here with us before we solve the case ... he may end up in jail. And Victoria will be lonely again."

"We'll solve this case all right!" Pearl said confidently. "In no time at all, you'll see!"

She could not have been more wrong in her assumption.

12

The next morning Victoria had breakfast with Pearl and me on the terrace, as she had done before on previous days. The early summer weather continued, and she didn't want to deviate from her habits just to have breakfast with Tim, who was tucked safely away inside the house. No one should get the idea that she was hosting a secret guest.

After she had long since finished her meal, and Pearl was also already full and taking a nap on her lap, Victoria suddenly jumped up, pushing the tiny one a little roughly to the side. She ran over to the fence—more precisely, to the garden gate through which one entered the Bruckhausens' park from our side.

Pearl let out an ill-tempered hiss at being disturbed, but then joined me. We both followed Victoria in order to see what she was up to.

We soon found out, because on the other side of the fence we spied Balduin Bruckhausen strolling aimlessly across the lawn. The old man often did that; he had repeatedly preached to his friend, my professor, about how important ten thousand steps a day were for longevity.

Victoria waved at him, prompting him to come over to the fence.

The two humans exchanged some small talk, but then

I realized what Victoria's intentions actually were. Seemingly casually, she mentioned Sinclair's murder to the old man, only to ask in the next sentence whether Balduin had heard any news from the police.

"How's the investigation going?" she inquired in a distinctly neutral tone.

The patriarch seemed all too ready to take up the topic. "Dreadful matter, isn't it? And our Tim, of all people—"

He shook his head. "I would never have believed him capable of such a thing, despite his previous, uh, missteps. When those policemen found the evidence, I said to Erwin that it all had to be a terrible misunderstanding. But then, what with his escape ... that's when Tim confirmed our suspicions, didn't he? I mean, if he were innocent, he wouldn't have just run away, he would have defended himself."

"What evidence are you talking about?" asked Victoria, looking at the old man in confusion.

"Didn't you hear? I thought the village gossip—" He waved his hand dismissively. "But you're still new in this community. I guess gossip doesn't reach you at maximum speed yet." He pursed his lips in a melancholy smile.

Then he readily gave her the information about what had happened: "Yesterday, the police searched for traces on the lakeshore and in our park, where Mr. McAllister had presumably been attacked, or rather killed. The forensics team were in your garden, too, weren't they?"

Victoria shook her head wordlessly.

"Well, maybe that wasn't entirely necessary," Balduin said, "after all, they found it by us."

"Found it?" echoed Victoria. By now she looked quite worried.

"That's what I'm saying," Balduin confirmed. "In our tool shed. After all, it's close to the water, practically the closest building to the shore. And Tim keeps his work tools there, of course."

"And that's where Sinclair was knocked out, or something? In the shed?"

"That's what it looks like, yes."

"What on earth was he doing there?" asked Victoria.

"Well, I'll get to that in a minute. The police have found it all out. The perpetrator—well, Tim, even though it still hasn't quite sunk in—cleaned the shed's floor after the deed was done. So at first glance there was nothing to see. But, you know, the police nowadays have all these modern methods at their disposal. And so they were able to make the traces of blood visible…. Yes, and then they also found the drugs. Well hidden, but not well enough."

"What *kind* of drugs?" Victoria's voice sounded shrill. I could smell how agitated she was.

"I don't quite remember, I'm afraid—something common. Cocaine? No, it wasn't that. But something like it. And the police found both Tim's and McAllister's fingerprints on the package. They also discovered a gun that had belonged to McAllister. He'd probably taken it to the meeting for self-defense, but it didn't do him any good. Tim knocked him down with the handle of a rake. He cleaned that up too, but again not well enough to fool the police. Well, after the attack I guess he carried McAllister down to the lake and drowned him there."

Balduin fell silent and stared sadly at the tips of his shoes.

I saw Victoria wiping her sweaty hands on the jeans she was wearing.

She swallowed, then asked the old man: "You said earlier that you never thought Tim would commit such a crime, despite his previous missteps. What did you mean by that? Does he have a criminal record?"

"You don't know about that?" He looked at her questioningly, but immediately corrected himself. "No, of course you don't, how could you? He certainly didn't advertise it, which is only too understandable. He didn't hide it from me at his job interview, though. He was very correct about it ... and I was willing to give him a chance. I thought he was a good man who had just made a slight mistake in his youth. That happens in the best of families, as they say, doesn't it? But now...."

He inhaled and exhaled heavily.

I watched Victoria struggle with herself. She didn't want to come across as a nosy gossip and keep probing, but at the same time she wanted—no, she needed—to know. Had to find out everything there was to know about the man she liked so much, and who was at the same time supposed to be a murderer.

"So what did Tim do?" she finally asked. "What does he have a criminal record for?"

Balduin slapped his hand to his forehead. "I'm such a senile old dodderer! Didn't I mention that? It was for drug possession. No, drug dealing, I think it was."

"Well, that fits all too perfectly with the drugs found in the tool shed," Victoria said in a brittle voice.

"Yes, doesn't it? And then the argument that Tim had with Sinclair ... of course, that speaks against him, too."

Eagerly, and at the same time already quite desperately, Victoria picked up this new cue. "What kind of argument?" she asked.

This time the old man didn't seem surprised that she had no idea of the matter in question. "Leon overheard the argument, or just bits and pieces of it. But it became clear that Tim and Sinclair couldn't stand each other, except for the drug deals they seemed to be doing."

"And what was the argument about?" Victoria probed.

The old man suddenly lowered his eyes in embarrassment. Again, the tips of his shoes seemed to be of the greatest interest to him. "Well, my dear, can't you guess? It was about you, I'm afraid."

"About *me*?" Victoria was starting to sound like one of those parrots that were so fond of repeating anything a two-legged said.

Balduin nodded. "Surely it hasn't escaped your notice that Tim likes you—very much? And so it was probably a thorn in his side that you preferred Sinclair to him."

Victoria started to protest: "But I didn't..."

She clasped her hands in front of her chest, and her breath became a sigh.

"A fight?" I said to Pearl. "Between Tim and Sinclair?

When is this supposed to have taken place?"

"Hmm, good question. I guess we weren't present. It's not like we were watching Tim round the clock—or Sinclair, for that matter."

"But Sinclair certainly wasn't after Victoria," I objected. "He was after the treasure that the professor was looking for when he was alive."

"I think so, too," Pearl said, "but Tim didn't know that. Remember the conversation you overheard, between him and the priest? Tim did let on to the father that he was jealous of Sinclair, didn't he?—because of Victoria."

I said nothing in reply. Pearl was right, but I was still convinced of Tim's innocence, even if the evidence the police had found could hardly be ignored.

Pearl once again managed to hit a sore spot: "At least now we know why Tim was so willing to take the chance I gave him to escape. He must have realized that things looked bad for him."

"Because he's guilty, you mean to say?"

"No, because he has a criminal record."

"I still can't believe it all," Balduin said into the silence that had fallen between the two humans. "Just terrible, the whole thing—"

He ran his hand through his hair, straightened his back, and mumbled something about having to take his leave. Erwin, his valet, was supposedly waiting for him with a few errands.

But Victoria held him back. "Please wait, Mr. Bruckhausen—Balduin. I wanted to ask you something else."

"Yes?" The old man raised his head, now looking

Victoria in the eye again.

I could tell she was only half-hearted about it, now that she had to see a murderer in Tim. Nevertheless, she went on to inquire about the Bruckhausens' family treasure that her father had been after before his death.

"Can you tell me more about it?" she asked the old man. "What is this treasure? Do you know what it contains? Are we talking about cash? Surely that would have lost its value by now."

Balduin threw a demonstrative glance at his wristwatch, probably to indicate that Victoria was already unduly taking up his time, but nevertheless he began to tell a story that he had surely recited many times before.

"My father, Artur Bruckhausen," he said, "was actually a staunch pacifist. In the first years of the war, the Nazis tried again and again to win him over to their cause, since he was a wealthy and very influential man. But he managed to stay out of the war effort for a long time. He made the essential donations that were expected of him, and showed up at certain political occasions, but in truth he did not have too high an opinion of Hitler and his dreams of world domination by the German race."

Pearl settled down in the grass, wrapping her tail around her hind paws. "Now where will this lead us?" she asked me.

I myself had pricked up my ears. Thanks to the professor I was a big fan of the subject of history. I found all the things the two-leggeds knew about their own past simply fascinating. We dogs had nothing like that; of course there were oral traditions among us, which included some ancient legends about our origins and distant past, but in truth the two-leggeds probably knew more about us than we did ourselves.

"However, in the last years of the war my father changed," Balduin continued his account. "I can't say exactly what tipped the scales—I never found out—but he did turn to the Nazis in the end. And he did so with great passion. I think it might have been because his two brothers, who had been on fire for the Nazi Empire right from the beginning, fell in battle during the war. They were killed by the Russians. From then on, Artur was no longer the same."

He paused for a moment, then added: "I have hardly any memory of my own of what I am telling you here. I was just a little boy at the time, and I couldn't make sense of half of what had happened back then until much later, long after my father's death. But anyway, in short, he became an ardent Nazi sympathizer at a time when the war seemed all but lost for the Germans. But my father and a group of other wealthy people here in our region believed in the *Endsieg*, the final victory, which was spoken about more and more often in German propaganda as the actual war effort went downhill. Father and his friends began to mobilize funds for the cause. And by funds I mean that they sold many of their valuables and hoarded their assets in gold and precious stones, the crisis currency par excellence. Then, when the war was officially lost and the Allied Forces invaded us, Father took it upon himself to find a safe hiding place for the accumulated treasure. The gold and the jewels were to be passed on to Hitler, in order to support his future seizure of power. But until that day, the Allied soldiers were not to be allowed to find the treasure under any circumstances."

"Hold on," Victoria interrupted. "Hitler died at the end of the war, didn't he? He took his own life, along with—what was her name, his girlfriend?—the two of them committed suicide in the Führer's bunker."

"If you believe the official historiography, yes," Balduin said. "But my father—and other Nazi regime sympathizers—believed in a conspiracy theory. You may have heard of that one, too; they were firmly convinced that Hitler had faked his own death. As you might know, all that was found of him afterwards were badly burned and therefore unrecognizable remains, presumably his and those of Eva Braun. She was his girlfriend—or rather wife, at the very end. In truth, my father believed Hitler had absconded to the New World, to Argentina. So it was a matter of keeping safe the treasure that was to go to the Führer on his return."

"I see," Victoria said. "That's quite a wild story. And how did the treasure end up disappearing? Was it stolen?"

"Oh no, nothing like that. It just happened that my father died very suddenly—he had an accident in his automobile and was killed on the spot, and thus he had no opportunity to reveal the treasure's hiding place to anyone. Also, during his lifetime he had become a very suspicious man. Paranoid, I guess you'd have to say. Not even his wife, my mother, knew where he had hidden the gold and jewels."

"Wow," said Victoria, "that's incredible! But it didn't cause your family financial hardship, I hope? Artur didn't put aside large parts of his fortune, did he?"

"What? Oh, no, that was not the case. We continued to be very wealthy, even after his death—and until the present day," he added with a smile that was probably meant to appear modest.

Then the old man glanced at his watch again, and before Victoria could hold him back any longer, he took his leave. She, on the other hand, remained standing by the hedge for a long time, as if frozen to the spot.

13

Throughout the rest of that day in our home, Victoria stayed out of Tim's way.

I could see that a storm was raging in her mind, and probably also in her heart. What she had learned about Tim had changed everything for her. I think she was still attracted to him—but she didn't trust him anymore.

"Has my knowledge of human nature failed miserably once again, Athos?" she asked me as she cleaned the entire house that afternoon, even though only a few days ago our cleaning lady had made everything shine. "Am I hiding a murderer in my house? Have I fallen in *love* with a murderer?"

"She's in love," reflected Pearl, ever the intrepid commentator. "That's good. After all, that's what we were going for, wasn't it?"

"It was, but..."

I paused, trying to figure out what I was going to say. "But now she thinks she's given her heart to a killer," I finally said. "That's anything but good."

Victoria's doubts, her emotional discord, didn't go unnoticed by Tim either.

After she had more or less successfully avoided him all day, devoting herself with great dedication to seemingly very important but in truth completely trivial activities such as cleaning the house, he approached her at dinner about her strange behavior.

"What's wrong?" he wanted to know, after Victoria had just served him—without a glance in his direction—some fried sausages with mashed potatoes. "You seem so ... I don't know, so closed off. Talk to me, Victoria. You can tell me anything. You know that, right?"

The atmosphere in the room was so tense that I could not even properly enjoy the smell of the sausages.

Victoria put down her cutlery, took a few nervous sips from her wine glass, then gave herself a visible jolt. She looked Tim firmly in the eye—and began to recount all that Balduin Bruckhausen had told her about the police investigation.

"Why didn't you mention a word about your criminal record?" she finally asked him, after she'd finished with her report.

He hesitated. Instead of answering he scratched Pearl, who jumped onto his lap in solidarity, behind the ears. Sometimes the pipsqueak didn't think exclusively about her next fish meal, but stood up for what was important to her. Even if it was a two-legged who was suspected of murder.

But Victoria didn't let up. "I can handle almost anything, I believe," she said in a grave voice, "but I sure as hell don't like being lied to."

"I didn't..." he began, but then he hesitated. "I just didn't want you to know. I wanted you to ... have a good impression of me. The very best."

"Of a drug dealer? Or what exactly are you, really?"

"Oh, God, Victoria. I was eighteen at the time—a

stupid kid who wanted to be cool. I picked the wrong friends, and yes, I was a drug addict for a while. And to be able to afford it, I sold the stuff myself, too. On a small scale! I wasn't a mob boss, if that's what you believe now. I was caught, and convicted. But I went to rehab—and I've never touched anything again, never even smoked a joint."

Victoria said nothing. I could smell how uncertain she was, but at the same time had the impression that she would have loved to hug Tim. That she wanted to tell him that his past didn't matter. But something inside her stopped her.

Suddenly she looked over at me as if to see if I was awake ... or rather, alert. Was she afraid that Tim would attack her?

Slowly and very quietly she asked him, "Did you murder Sinclair McAllister?"

14

The next morning Pearl woke me up by hitting my nose with one of her miniature paws. She liked to do that, calling it a tender gesture when I complained about it ... but this time I didn't even get to protest.

"Tim is gone!" she told me, after barely having startled me from my sleep. "I've looked everywhere—and the freshest trail leads into the hall, to the front door. He's run away, Athos."

We had spent the night in Victoria's room, while Tim had stayed in the guest room once more. At some point during the night he must have stolen away without any of us noticing.

"What do you think it means?" asked Pearl. "Is he guilty after all?"

"Maybe he's just offended that Victoria doesn't trust him anymore?" I suggested.

"Hmm, also possible," Pearl agreed. "But it really wasn't smart of him not to tell her about the criminal record. And what the police found in that shed ... the bloodstains, the drug package with his fingerprints on it—it doesn't look good for him, does it?"

"No," I grumbled. It really didn't. "Let's give him some time, and then I'll look for him again, okay? Maybe I can get him to come back."

"If he chooses the same hiding place again as when he

first escaped," Pearl said.

"Do you think I should go after him right away? While the trail is fresh? In case he's headed somewhere else."

"No," said Pearl. "I think we need to find the real killer before Tim can return to Victoria. Before that, I don't think it's going to work out between the two of them."

One could think whatever one wanted to about the midget, but sometimes she came up with fairly clever ideas.

Victoria slept late that morning, drank the first cup of coffee right after getting up, and only then did she shuffle to Tim's guest room. There she found out what we already knew—namely that he had run away. This plunged her into emotional chaos once again.

When the doorbell suddenly shrilled, a sharp cry escaped her.

She laced up the robe that had been hanging limply from her shoulders, looked around for me again as if she needed a protector, then walked towards the hall.

By now I felt like her personal bodyguard, although I had been concentrating lately on helping Victoria to find happiness in love. It was not a role change that I liked; from Cupid to Cerberus, so to speak.

But of course I couldn't chicken out either. So I followed Victoria and walked with her to the door. She opened it timidly. But straight away she relaxed and let her shoulders sink. Sabrina was standing outside on the doormat.

She had a plate of cookies with her, which she handed to Victoria. "Am I interrupting? May I come in for a moment?"

Victoria stepped aside, and I toddled off as well so Sabrina wouldn't have to climb over me.

"I'm not here for another session," Sabrina explained as she followed Victoria into the living room. There the two women settled down at the table and Sabrina took back one of the cookies she had brought Victoria as a gift.

My human was too distracted, with her thoughts probably still too much on Tim, to offer her guest coffee or anything else. But Sabrina was not bothered by this. She immediately began to talk about the reason for her visit.

"I've made up my mind!" she announced, beaming. What a contrast to Victoria, who looked as if she had just been beaten up.

"Made up your mind?" my human repeated, without any real interest.

"Yes! About Adrian! I'm going to marry him. I wanted you to be one of the first to know, since you have helped me so much. Thanks to you, I managed to make a clear decision, and I'm going to stand by it. I love Adrian, you know—more than Leon. And he's a better match for me. That became very clear to me during our conversation a few days ago. So I wanted to thank you again for your help and advice."

She shoved the plate of cookies right under Victoria's nose, and our poor human finally let herself be persuaded to put one of the delicacies into her mouth.

Pearl jumped on the table with a meow that meant something like, "Can I have a taste, too?"

She didn't wait for an answer, of course—before Victoria could shoo her away, she had already sunk her tiny fangs into one of the cookies and pulled it off the plate. In the next moment she had disappeared under the table and started to devour her prey.

"You're so greedy, Tiny!" I reprimanded her.

"Am not," she shot back, her voice mingled with smacking sounds.

"Are too! You're going to get all fat and round!"

"Pah, I have a great figure! Unlike a certain Malamute who always likes to blame his thick fur."

I couldn't let her get away with such impudence. Diving under the table, barking wildly, I chased Pearl out from underneath it and gave the cheeky house tiger a blow from my paw. A tender one of course; I'm not a brute after all.

Needless to say, Pearl still complained as if I had torn her to pieces, and I ended up earning a reprimand from Victoria.

"Don't be so rough, Athos," she called to me. "Don't hurt Pearl!" However, she didn't say a word about the midget's cookie theft.

Life really was unfair.

15

My human turned back to her guest. Only now did Victoria seem to slowly process what Sabrina had told her with such glee.

"So you're going to marry Adrian? How nice, I'm happy for you—and for him as well. Congratulations!"

"You're invited to the wedding, of course," said Sabrina. "Although we haven't set a firm date yet."

"I'm very pleased to hear that," Victoria said. "Really nice of you."

It almost broke my heart to hear how sad she sounded. She must have been thinking of her own dreams of love, which had been burst like a soap bubble in the last twenty-four hours.

Sabrina chattered along happily for quite a while, talking about bridal fashions, possible destinations for the honeymoon and whether the wedding ceremony should take place in the family mansion or somewhere else.

Victoria listened quietly, nodding at the appropriate intervals, but finally she found her own voice again—seemingly remembering that there was still a murder case to be solved. It could only mean that she wasn't entirely convinced of Tim's guilt after all. At least there was a ray of hope.

She began by asking Sabrina about the Bruckhausens' treasure. "I get the impression that Sinclair McAllister was looking for it," she added as an explanation for her interest. "Maybe that's why he was killed."

Sabrina's eyes widened. "What makes you think that? He was murdered by our gardener over some drugs. At least that's what the police think. And I mean, Tim's escape ... it confirms it, doesn't it?"

"I don't know," Victoria said. There was uncertainty in her gaze, but at the same time determination. She had apparently decided to get to the bottom of the murder mystery herself.

That's good, I thought.

Victoria repeated her question about the treasure. "You are a budding historian, Sabrina," she said, "so surely you know quite a bit about your family mystery? It must be fascinating to have such a secret in your immediate circle."

"Your father was looking for the treasure," Sabrina replied. "He asked me a lot of questions about it, in the last few weeks before he died. But I'm sure you know that. I think he did a lot more digging into it than I've been able to do so far. I mean, of *course* I'm interested in our family history, but I just don't have enough time. Studying keeps me pretty busy. And then, lately, there's been my love life as well" she added with another blissful smile.

"Do you perhaps remember what you told my father specifically about the treasure, when he asked you about it?" Victoria wanted to know.

"Hmm, nothing really useful, I'm afraid. I told him that I suspected the hiding place was nearby. My great-grandfather Artur did not travel while he was gathering and eventually hiding the treasure. That much is clear from his correspondence at the time, according to my granddad. I also said to your father that the hiding place is probably very small. After all gold and jewels, even if they have great value, don't really need much space. But these are all obvious points, aren't they? As I've said, I'm afraid I wasn't much help to your father in his search. It didn't discourage him, though."

A melancholy smile suddenly flitted across Sabrina's face. "I miss the professor, you know. He was very kind, and I really liked him; I'm not exaggerating when I say that he inspired me to study history. He always told me about his research in such an exciting way, and often recommended books to me, which I then literally devoured—"

"Did you get the impression that he had changed?" Victoria interrupted her. "In the days before his death?"

"Changed? Hmm, yes, quite possibly. He seemed worried the last time I met him, which was not his usual manner. I only ever knew him as a very cheerful person—always full of energy and positive in every way."

Victoria leaned forward. "And what was he worried about?" she asked.

"Do you think I could steal another cookie?" Pearl asked, distracting me.

"Shh, listen," I protested, "the things these two are discussing now could turn out to be important."

"I am listening," Pearl said. "I can use my ears and eat something at the same time. Can't you?"

I put my muzzle on her back, holding her down on the ground.

"You're not going to interrupt the conversation with a cookie theft now," I said. "Nor are you going to howl like a puppy so Victoria thinks I'm a brute again!" I quickly added when she tried to defend herself.

Much to my astonishment, Pearl complied for once. She forced herself out from under my muzzle, but then lay down next to me and used my front paw as a pillow. She liked doing that, and it probably represented an act of grace towards me in her eyes, apart from the fact that I made for a very comfortable cushion.

"I really can't say what your father was worried about," Sabrina told Victoria. "I only met him briefly that day, the last time I saw him—I think it was the day before he died. But I remember he dropped a strange remark. He said, *Isn't it terrible how money, or the greed for it, corrupts even the best of people?* I couldn't make any sense of that."

"Sounds like it was about the treasure, too," Victoria said.

"Huh, yeah, quite possibly."

For a little while neither woman said a word.

Then Sabrina shook her head. "My great-grandfather Artur must have been a really strange guy. I've often thought so—I mean, how do you go from being a staunch pacifist to an ardent Nazi sympathizer? What must have been going on in his head? What with his dream of final victory, and the treasure he hid to pass on to the Führer later on, he almost brought our family to ruin. And then there was his paranoia, which kept him from confiding a single word to anyone about the hiding place of the gold and jewels. The years after his death were very hard for my great-grandmother—Balduin's mother. It wasn't until my grandfather grew up and finally took over the family business that things started to improve again. He was a born businessman from the beginning, and he's always been there for the family. He really has done great things, even though he's been dogged by misfortune. His first wife suffered a fatal accident at an early age, and you know, I think she was Balduin's great love. He doesn't often talk about her, but when he does you can tell how painful the loss still is for him today."

"Did he never remarry?" asked Victoria.

"Yes, he did. He had his children with his second wife: Amalia and Maxim, and my mother—who unfortunately has already passed away. She had cancer, you know. And Grandpa would certainly have liked to have had even more children. As I said, he's a real family man. Whenever there's a birth in the family, he is always beside himself with joy. But then his second wife also passed away ... he really has been dogged by misfortune."

"I'm so sorry to hear that," Victoria said sympathetically. "I also get the impression that he is completely absorbed in his family. He seems very happy with all of you—and he does, after all, take an active part in your lives."

"Oh yes, he does," Sabrina said. "Sometimes he

meddles a little too much for my taste, but he really means well. And that's the way parents—or grandparents—are, isn't it?"

Victoria nodded wordlessly.

She seemed lost in thought for a moment, then she asked Sabrina another question: "How did your family actually acquire their wealth? I don't even know what business you're in. I mean your grandfather. Or Artur—how did he amass this fortune that he was going to donate to Hitler?"

Sabrina furrowed her brow. "I can't tell you that exactly either. We've never produced anything, or traded in goods. Pursuing a conventional job was frowned upon back then ... heck, it still is today, if you talk to my grandfather. It's always been about fiscal dealings in our family: transactions on the stock market and investments in companies.... That's how it was from the beginning, and that's how it still is. My grandpa is a real financial genius."

She smiled, then rose from the table. "But now I've kept you long enough, dear Victoria. I really just wanted to—to share my joy with you."

"I'm very happy for you," Victoria affirmed. "But before you go, I have one more question: did my father perhaps say something to you about the grave of a young woman, at the church cemetery? Käthe Küpper, that was her name. It's the grave that was recently broken open."

She did not add that it had probably been Sinclair McAllister who had committed the outrage.

"Yes, your father wanted to know about Käthe," Sabrina said. "Why do you ask?"

"Do you know who she was? Maybe an, um, mistress of your great-grandfather?"

"What? Oh no, not a love affair. Käthe was his childhood sweetheart. She died when my great-grandfather was still a very young man, and I think he loved her madly. I believe she came from humble beginnings, and it was Artur who had that magnificent tomb with the guardian angel built for her."

"And does the name *Hathor* mean anything to you, in connection with this woman?" Victoria continued. "My father recorded it several times in his notes. Supposedly, Artur referred to this Hathor as his greatest treasure. It is said to have been a kind of pet name for Käthe."

"I've never heard of it," Sabrina replied with a shrug. "As I've said, I'm sure your father ended up knowing a lot more about my family's history than I do myself. But Hathor could very well be a pet name. Do you know who Hathor is?"

"No—should I?"

"I guess it's not a gap in education for a psychologist," Sabrina said with a slightly patronizing grin. "Hathor is, if you will, the Egyptian precursor to Venus. A goddess of love ... it's a very romantic pet name for a beloved woman, don't you think? Perhaps this Käthe Küpper reminded my great-grandfather of the goddess Hathor for some reason. I guess we'll never know."

"You know what we should be asking ourselves?" Pearl meowed to me after Sabrina had left, and she'd captured another cookie. At least this time she was generous enough to share the treat with me.

"What?" I asked, as I indulged in the sugar shock with some appetite.

"Sinclair broke open that grave, the one belonging to Käthe Küpper. And old Artur gave her romantic pet names and called her his greatest treasure. What if he hid his *monetary* treasure, that is, the gold and jewels for Hitler's return, under her grave's ledger stone? Surely no one would have looked for it there."

"That's probably the idea Sinclair had, too," I said, "and the reason why he broke it open."

"Yes, exactly. But what if he actually *found* the treasure inside? What if he was murdered because of it—because someone wanted to take all the gold and jewels away from him?"

16

Victoria did some work in our garden until lunchtime. It was probably some kind of occupational therapy for her—did it bring her mentally closer to Tim, the gardener, at the same time?

Pearl was sunbathing on a flat stone, while I was trying to lend Victoria a helping paw by digging around the flower beds a bit. But she—as always when I indulged in excavation work—got in my way.

"Athos, stop it! Why do you want to keep digging those holes? You're a sled dog, not a vole!"

I didn't even try to tell her how many advantages digging had, or above all what fun it was.

"Maybe you should try it some time?" I suggested to her. "It would be a great new form of therapy for your clients. And for you, too," I added as an afterthought. Victoria was someone who now desperately needed psychological support.

Of course, as usual I was neither heard nor understood.

As we sat down on the terrace to a small meal a short while later, loud voices from the neighbor's garden drifted over to us. I pricked up my ears and ran to the hedge. Pearl followed me, of course, scurrying right between my legs in her excitement, almost bringing me down.

On the mansion's driveway we spotted Balduin Bruck-hausen, who was talking to our village doctor, Guido Rauch. Or rather, the two men were arguing—and quite loudly, too.

I was just about to duck through the hedge and stalk closer to them when a call from Victoria stopped me. "Stay here, Athos! This seems to be a private conversation. You have no business there, even if you can't understand anything," she added.

What a philistine! But at least she had also noticed the two men. And I could have sworn that she herself was pricking up her ears to hear what they were arguing about, even if she had remained sitting on the terrace.

So I played the good dog and stayed on our side of the hedge. Pearl joined me—can you believe it? Normally she turned a deaf ear whenever Victoria gave us an order, and always got off with a half-hearted reprimand afterwards. Because she was so cute and you couldn't be angry with her ... you know how it goes.

I didn't have to eavesdrop for long before I understood what the argument between Guido and Balduin was about: Amalia. Guido was suggesting to the patriarch that they celebrate a double wedding—Sabrina with Adrian and he himself with Amalia. Apparently he'd wanted to marry Balduin's widowed daughter for a long time, because the subject didn't seem to be a new one.

The old man, however, didn't want to hear about a double wedding, nor about a marriage between the doctor and Amalia in principle.

The two men continued to exchange words for quite a

while, becoming more and more unpleasant, then finally Guido left the property with a red face and at a run, while Balduin, who'd turned the same color, returned to the mansion.

"Do you think this has anything to do with Sinclair's murder?" Pearl asked me.

"Hmm, I can't imagine so," I said.

But Pearl was not so easily convinced. "I'd bet my magnificent fluffy tail that the killer is to be found over there in that mansion," she said. "I mean, Sinclair was bumped off in the Bruckhausens' tool shed. Surely no stranger could have strayed in there. And we're still convinced that Tim isn't a killer, aren't we?"

"We are," I confirmed, although deep in my soul I perhaps no longer fully believed in the gardener's innocence.

"We need an insider in the mansion, an undercover spy—in short, me," Pearl announced, sounding like a miniature wannabe secret agent.

I couldn't help but think of the movies I'd seen a few times on TV. They were about a master spy named James Bond, who had the identification number 007 and always fortified himself for his adventures with a glass of martini. Shaken, not stirred.

Just for one insane moment, I saw Pearl in front of me, with dark sunglasses on her tiny nose, whispering to a waiter, "The fish grilled, please, not breaded."

Victoria's voice snapped me out of my ludicrous fantasy. "Come on, little ones, let's go inside. I think it's about to rain."

She began to collect the plates from her repast and walked into the house with them.

Pearl looked at me, then followed her. She didn't like rain; the little diva couldn't stand it when her gorgeous white coat got wet.

I sniffed and looked up at the sky. It was possible that Victoria was right, and rain was indeed on the way. I didn't mind, of course, but I followed my human and the midget into the house anyway.

After Victoria had washed the few dishes and dried her hands, she stood around indecisively in her kitchen.

"So what now?" she wondered aloud. "Does it even make sense to keep trying to solve Sinclair's murder? I mean, I already know who killed him, don't I?"

She gave me a dispirited look and then picked Pearl up from the floor. She pressed the tiny one against her cheek and let out a dejected sigh.

"You mustn't give up," I told Victoria, giving her a devoted head butt against her thigh. At least I made her laugh.

For a moment she was still standing there, lost, but then she pulled herself together and returned to the library, immersing herself once more in her father's documents.

She worked with full concentration, reading old letters, diaries, and loose notes, and also turned on the professor's old laptop again.

"Dad really was the classic absent-minded professor," she said at one point with a theatrical sigh. "A real slob; his notes are so scattered and jumbled—"

She paused in mid-sentence, squinted her eyes, and stared at the open double-page spread of the notebook she had in front of her.

"That's really strange," she grumbled. "This is about a death ... about the death of Amalia's husband, to be exact. He died of food poisoning, it seems. A spoiled fish dish? Sounds bad—but did my father really think someone might have tampered with it? He doesn't spell it out in so many words, but one could almost get the impression—why did he write something down about this death in particular? Surely it can't be of historical interest. Hmm. Was he playing detective, or what?"

She raised her head, fixing me with a penetrating stare. As always when she was alone but urgently needed someone to talk to, she chatted with me.

I signaled she had my attention with a faithful expression and excited panting. "Death?" I asked. "A poisoning? You should take a closer look!"

"Why did this bother my father?" she mused further. "And not for the first time, it seems to me. I've already read a similar thread of e-mail correspondence on his laptop. My father had an exchange with a colleague at the university, from the medical faculty—and he asked about this very thing—fish poisoning. And just earlier I found some notes that dealt with the death of Sabrina's father. He also died very young, the victim of a hunting accident. What does this have to do with the treasure that my Dad was actually looking for? Can you explain it to me?"

I could not.

"Fish poisoning?" Pearl repeated, startled. Her whiskers were vibrating.

"I'm sure your salmon is perfectly safe," I assured her.

"I should hope so." She sat down on her fluffy rear end. "Well, luckily I have Victoria as my taster. So I shouldn't be in any danger."

"Really ... you're impossible!" I reproached her.

Pearl began to clean her paws. "Anyway," she said, "apparently I'm in the right again. Something's not quite in order over there with the Bruckhausens. We need to bring in an undercover agent!"

The possible dangers of eating fish were forgotten. In the pipsqueak's blue eyes was flaring the spirit of adventure.

17

Pearl wasted no time putting her plan into action.

"I have the perfect idea as to how to infiltrate the Bruckhausens' mansion," she informed me as we returned to the garden late that afternoon and spied Amalia over the hedge on the lawn with her children.

"Pearl Bond, Spy 008, with a license to devour salmon," I commented—for which I earned an amused look from the cat. She apparently knew the movies, too, and she seemed to enjoy taking the role of secret agent very much.

The rain clouds had cleared again, without a single drop having fallen, and the sun was blazing from the sky as if we had traveled forward in time to July.

Amalia had gathered her entire flock of children in the garden. The smallest lay on a blanket in the grass and was taking up his mother's full attention. She was stroking and caressing the child, making sounds rather like a lovesick duck.

When I gazed at Amalia more intently, I noticed that she looked very depressed. She must even have been crying, because her eyes were red and her eyelids swollen.

The somewhat larger middle child was crawling around on the meadow, and had just been eating an earthworm.

Marlene had just been playing with her dolls, but when Pearl crossed the hedge and ran purposefully towards her the plastic figures were immediately forgotten.

I couldn't believe my eyes: Pearl was snuggling into the girl's arms, purring loudly. The little hypocrite!

"A good investigator has to make sacrifices," she told me, surrendering to the little girl's caresses with stoic heroism.

I quickly realized what she was up to, and her plan worked out perfectly. When Amalia got up after a while and collected her children in order to return to the house, Marlene pressed the tiny cat against her.

"Can I take the kitten into the house, Mom?" she pleaded. "Look, she's so comfortable with me. Oh please say yes!"

Amalia herself seemed surprised that Pearl was letting herself be cuddled so willingly today. She certainly loved her daughter dearly, but at the same time she was aware of how exhausting the little girl could be.

"My dear," she said, "you'll have to ask our kind neighbor. Pearl is her cat, after all." She spoke loud enough for Victoria, who was sitting in our garden brooding to herself, to take notice.

Marlene immediately came running to the hedge, holding Pearl tightly in her little arms, and repeated her request without any hesitation or shyness.

"Victoria? Can I take Pearl with me? Just for a few hours. Oh please, please!"

Victoria looked puzzled. She, too, seemed surprised

that Pearl suddenly seemed to have a crush on the girl, when usually she avoided her. Now, however, Pearl pressed her head against Marlene's neck and purred like a royal tigress.

"Well," Victoria said, "from the looks of it I think Pearl likes being with you. So of course you can take her with you. But, um, if she wants to leave again, you have to let her out of the house, okay? And otherwise, please bring her back to me no later than this evening. Agreed?"

"I promise!" squeaked Marlene. "Oh, thank you so much!"

Pearl's first mission as an undercover investigator went like clockwork. After sunset, I was already waiting for her impatiently—and Victoria also looked quite relieved when she came trudging into the living room through the cat door, just in time for dinner.

Of course she had to fortify herself first after her adventure, but right after she'd eaten her fill we retreated to the front of the tiled stove. I didn't like it as warm as the midget, but of course I wasn't asked, as usual.

"So, what did you find out?" I probed impatiently.

"Hmm," Pearl said cryptically. "I was able to overhear two conversations. But whether they have anything to do with Sinclair's murder...." Her ears were twitching with dissatisfaction.

"Why don't you tell me," I suggested.

"Okay. So right after Amalia went into the house with her brood, she decided to video-call the doctor. From her laptop."

"Guido Rauch, the village doctor?"

"Exactly—she's terribly in love with the guy. And he with her."

"We already know that," I interjected, perhaps a little impatiently.

I'd secretly hoped that Pearl would return with information that would allow us to clear Tim of the terrible suspicion of murder. But how our neighbors' love affairs would help us in this regard, I could not imagine for the life of me.

"So the doctor and Amalia want to get married," Pearl continued, "but Balduin forbids it. And that's why Guido wants Amalia to flee with him, along with the children. Elopement, he called it. *Let's elope together, like they'd have done a hundred years ago*! he said to her."

"Such a plan actually seems kind of old-fashioned to me," I said. "On the other hand, Balduin interfering with their marriage plans like that ... you only see that kind of thing in historical movies these days. I don't understand why Amalia puts up with it."

"Well, she made that pretty clear in the video call with the doctor," Pearl replied. "She's living off Balduin's money, and in quite a princely fashion, too. And I guess she doesn't feel like having to work herself."

"But the doctor—" I objected.

"He earns reasonably well ... for a country doctor," Pearl said, as if she were an expert on the financial status of human occupations. "He pointed that out several times in the phone call. Apparently he's the third generation in his family to run the practice in our village. It would be hard for him to give up his patients here, but he'd do it—for Amalia, if the two of them ran away together. They both know that Balduin would make their lives hell if they defied his will and then stayed here in our neighborhood. So they would have to move to another part of the country, where Guido would have to set up a new practice. But there's plenty of sick people everywhere, I should think."

"Does mean they're planning to leave? Did they say when?"

"Wait, it's not that simple," Pearl said, slowing me down. "Amalia wants to be with Guido, but she also loves her father very much. *After all, he only means well for me,* she told Guido. *And if you give up your practice here and have to start over, what are we going to live on?*"

"Good question," I said. "She might be worried about how she'll be able to feed her children then. That's probably more important to her than marrying Guido."

"Looks like it. The doctor said: Don't you trust me to take care of you? And she said, Yes, but what if something happened to you? Like it did to my first husband? A misfortune can always strike ... and then the children and I will be left with nothing!"

"Hmm, that sounds almost as complicated as Tim and Victoria's situation," I said. "Since she's come to believe that he's a murderer."

Pearl agreed and lowered her head onto my paw. "Yeah, looks like they won't be eloping after all, at least for now."

"And what else do you have to report?" I asked. "Did you discover anything that might have to do with Sinclair's murder?"

"I don't know. But I certainly don't have to tell you that two-leggeds commit murder for just such mundane reasons: because they're unhappy in love, for example."

"Yeah, right. But what could Sinclair have to do with Amalia and the doctor's love crisis?"

Pearl didn't know the answer to that, either.

She then told me about another conversation she had overheard. "Of course, after Amalia's video phone call with the doctor, I immediately ducked out of her rooms there at the mansion. Not that Marlene, that horrible child, would have groped me any further. I tromped around the house, looking for the other two-leggeds living there ... and I finally came across Balduin having a conversation with his grandson, Fabius. And again, it was about marriage, which must be a popular topic among the Bruckhausens."

"Fabius wants to get married, too?" I asked. "But to whom?"

"He doesn't want to, he's *supposed* to," Pearl said. "At least if Balduin has his way. Apparently the old man isn't against marriage in general; rather the opposite. I guess he longs for more offspring, for great-grandchildren. *Starting a family is true happiness.* That's what he was preaching to Fabius. And that he's already at the right age for it."

"And how did Fabius take it?"

"He was relaxed, as always. Nothing really upsets him that easily. He said he had nothing against a woman in principle; he just doesn't want any children ... he said they're so much work."

"He's not wrong about that," I said.

Pearl agreed with a passionate meow. "Yeah, who would volunteer to have a little monster like that Marlene kid?"

She began to groom herself thoroughly, as if her fur were still in disarray from the little girl's copious displays of affection.

"Now I really don't understand what Balduin has against the doctor," I mused to myself, while Pearl was still devoting herself to grooming. "After all, if he is such a family man, why can't Amalia marry again?"

"Maybe Guido is not rich enough, not respected enough?" the midget speculated. "The Bruckhausens are quite full of themselves, aren't they? They think they're better than everyone else."

"The doctor is certainly *respected*, though," I objected. "At least around here. But maybe not rich...."

"There you have it," Pearl said with satisfaction.

"But Leon—whom Sabrina wanted to marry originally—is neither respectable nor rich, is he? And Balduin had no objections to a marriage between those two. Apart from the fact that now Adrian has gotten in the way. Besides, the Bruckhausens really are rich enough themselves."

"People never think they're rich enough," Pearl replied in her philosopher's voice.

I could not object to that. And I had no real desire to rack my brains any further about the intricate family relationships of our neighbors.

Sinclair's death had to do with the Bruckhausens' treasure—that still seemed to me the best explanation for his murder. Not about who loved whom, and who was or wasn't allowed to marry.

I left Pearl by the warm tiled stove and strolled over to the terrace doors. They were closed now, but on the floor directly in front of them it was at least somewhat cooler than in the rest of the room.

But I was not to be granted the blessing of a peaceful nap. When I had almost dozed off, a loud bang suddenly shattered the stillness of the evening.

A gunshot!

18

I was immediately on the tips of my paws—and Pearl and Victoria also jumped up. Our human crossed the room quickly, and the midget and I zoomed after her. She ran into the hall, but there she hesitated to open the front door. Instead, she stopped and listened.

The shot had come from that direction: from the street in front of our property, in fact, which one reached when leaving the house through the main entrance. Victoria's modest human hearing had not deceived her about that ... and now, suddenly, angry voices could be heard outside. Two-leggeds in a panic. A man—whose voice I recognized—was screaming for help. It was Balduin Bruckhausen.

Victoria didn't dare leave the house. Instead she turned to her handbag, which was sitting on a dresser in the hall, and dug out her cell phone.

She must have dialed the emergency services, because right away she made a report to the person on the other end of the line that a shot had been fired on our street.

"Please, come quickly!" she cried breathlessly into the phone. "Our neighbor—he may have been attacked. I'm sure I heard a shot outside my house. And a scream. I don't dare look myself; the shooter could still be around here somewhere!"

The man on the phone seemed to confirm to her that

this was a reasonable precaution and that she should not leave the house until the police officers arrived. They would be on their way immediately.

So we waited idly for a few minutes, until two police cars arrived with their sirens wailing and blue lights flashing.

Only then did Victoria dare to open the front door and run to the garden gate. Pearl and I followed her, of course. In the excitement she forgot to put a leash on us, so once outside we could check for ourselves what had actually happened.

Apart from the three police officers in uniform, I spotted Balduin Bruckhausen leaning against the hood of one of the police cars, apparently giving an officer a report on what he had observed. He was talking in a shrill voice, ruffling his hair again and again, and seemed very agitated.

Beside him I recognized Dr. Guido Rauch, who was trying to calm the old man down and apparently also wanted to find out whether he was injured.

"There's nothing wrong with me," Balduin snapped at the doctor indignantly. "But Adrian, he's—dead!" He broke off, his face contorted in agony, and he made a nervous gesture with his hand in the direction of the opposite sidewalk.

Only then did I realize that there was a dead person lying on the pavement. It was Adrian Seeberg, as Balduin had already indicated.

I ran over to the body, with Pearl in tow, but one of the policemen intervened before we could reach him.

"Hey, whose are these two?" the man in uniform exclaimed.

Victoria came running up.

"Mine," she confessed, mumbling an apology. Then she waved her arms wildly and called our names.

"Athos, Pearl! Here!" she ordered.

Pearl and I pulled back a bit and stood a few meters away from the body.

That Adrian was dead was obvious even from this distance. There was still a residue in the air of the acrid stench that human guns give off when they are fired, and there was a gaping hole in Adrian's chest. A pool of blood had already formed on the sidewalk around him.

Dr. Guido Rauch came hurrying over to Victoria. He seemed to want to make himself useful in some way after having been so coldly rebuffed by Balduin.

"Are you all right?" he asked her.

At that moment, another scream tore through the night. The smell of human fear and despair wafted into my nose.

Sabrina came running towards us from the Bruckhausens' mansion, or rather towards the dead Adrian—whose corpse she had apparently just spotted, hence her scream.

Leon was following closely behind her, and caught up with her and stopped her before the policeman guarding the body could get in her way, as he had done with us.

Leon pulled Sabrina into his arms and tried to cover her eyes.

"Don't look, honey!" he cried. "Don't inflict that sight upon yourself. There's nothing you can do for him!"

He himself peered over at his motionless competitor still lying in the pool of blood, and his eyes widened. He seemed to have realized that no one could do anything for Adrian anymore.

"Please stay back," the police officer said.

"Is he dead?" Leon asked the man straightforwardly.

The officer confirmed it—and Sabrina emitted a howl that would have done credit to a wolf.

Victoria ran up to Sabrina, put her hand on her arm and began to talk softly to her, while Leon, for his part, was still holding her tightly.

Our human murmured a few words of sympathy, but could not take her own eyes off the corpse. "I was in the house," she said tonelessly, addressing no one in particular. "I heard the shot and dialed the emergency number."

The doctor hurried the few steps over to us and nodded with a somber expression. "I heard the shot, too—and right after that, Mr. Bruckhausen's scream. I, um, happened to be nearby, so I ran over right away."

"Then you were braver than me," Victoria said.

"Not at all," he quickly objected. "It was probably foolish of me. I didn't think; I just reacted on reflex. I could have walked into the middle of a shootout."

He pressed his lips together, only now seeming to realize the danger he had exposed himself to.

"Were you ... able to see who did this?" asked Victoria. The doctor shook his head. "Balduin didn't see anything either; he already told the policemen that. He was walking with Adrian when it happened, just a few steps behind him. The sidewalk is pretty narrow here, isn't it? The two of them were on their way home from the pub. I think the shot came from over there in the woods. At least, that's what it sounded like."

He pointed with his hand to the little wood that formed the end of our street, and bordered on the overgrown part of the Bruckhausens' park.

"Oh God, Sabrina," the doctor added. "I'm so sorry!"

The young woman was crying bitterly now, struggling for breath between heartrending sobs. Leon held her in his arms; otherwise she would probably have collapsed and fallen to the ground.

A new siren blared, and another vehicle with blue lights drove up and stopped at the side of the road. It was an ambulance, from which two paramedics emerged. One of the policemen ran towards them to put them in the picture about what had happened.

Leon looked around without letting go of Sabrina. He turned his head and stared into the dark forest behind him. "It must have been that gardener again," he exclaimed in a voice filled with hatred. "He's taken another victim!"

"I said from the beginning that the guy is a bad apple," a creaky voice joined the conversation. It was Erwin, the valet. He had also found his way here from the mansion in the meantime, from whence the shot and Balduin's piercing cry for help must have been heard almost as clearly as in our own house.

Victoria glared angrily at the valet and took Tim's side. "What reason could he have had to shoot Adrian?" she protested.

But Erwin was not impressed. He merely shrugged. "Does a psychopath like him need any reason? These lunatics kill, find pleasure in it, and then do it again...."

One of the policemen approached our group and asked us to return to the other side of the street or, even better, to our houses. He took down the names of everyone present and announced that more detailed testimony would be taken later.

Victoria offered to accompany Sabrina home. Leon, however, seemed only too eager to take care of Sabrina himself, and to offer her comfort, so our human turned to Balduin next. He, in turn, was having a bad-tempered discussion with one of the paramedics. In a loud voice he was insisting that nothing was wrong with him and that he did not need medical attention.

"I'm a psychotherapist," Victoria told the paramedic, "I'll take care of my neighbor."

The young man seemed relieved. "Oh yes, that's fine. That's kind of you."

So finally we all walked over to the Bruckhausens together. Pearl and I trotted along behind the two-leggeds.

"Why did Adrian have to die?" Pearl asked as we were walking side by side. "How does his death fit in with the murder of Sinclair?"

I had not the slightest idea.

At the mansion we were met by Amalia and Marlene;

the two youngest children had probably slept through the commotion. Guido, who had also followed us, immediately turned to his beloved—and this time Balduin was too distracted to make any protest.

The old man was leaning heavily on Victoria's arm, and he let her lead him into the Bruckhausens' kitchen. There she placed him in one of the chairs around a large dining table and asked Erwin to put on some tea. For once the servant did as he was told. He seemed concerned for his employer, saying several times, "Please don't get upset, Mr. Bruckhausen. Think of your heart!"

Sabrina, Leon, Amalia, Marlene and Guido also settled down at the table, and finally Erwin served each of them a cup of tea. Pearl and I ensconced ourselves under the table.

Balduin began—without anyone prompting him—to recount the events of the evening.

"Adrian and I met with Father Valentin, at the Black Man Inn. We were talking to him about Sabrina and Adrian's wedding, as there were quite a lot of preparations to be made regarding the church ceremony."

He shook his head, sniffling. "Now the poor child is a widow even before she could walk down the aisle." He sounded terribly angry, and pounded his fist on the table so hard that the wood groaned.

Then he looked over at Sabrina, who'd sunk against Leon's shoulder and closed her eyes. She didn't seem to be aware that her grandfather was talking about her. Balduin uttered a low wail and seemed very distraught.

I knew the inn that the old man had mentioned. My

professor had also eaten there often and with great pleasure. It was perhaps ten minutes away from our house at a human's walking pace.

I personally didn't like the Black Man very much; it was always terribly hot and stuffy in there. But at least the landlord was a dog lover who always served me fresh water and a few treats from the kitchen.

"Please calm down, Mr. Bruckhausen," Erwin intervened again. "Would you like a piece of cake with your tea?"

"I don't want any damn cake right now!" the old man grumbled.

Erwin glanced at Guido, who was sitting close to Amalia but had not spoken a word until now. "Isn't there anything you can do for Mr. Bruckhausen, Doctor? A sedative, perhaps?"

Balduin jumped up. "I'm going to bed!" he announced abruptly. He apparently didn't want to know about any sedative.

With his departure, the rest of the group dissolved as well. Leon led Sabrina out of the room—although, unlike Balduin, they at least said goodbye to the others. The doctor and Amalia also rose, gave each other meaningful looks, but then stood around indecisively. It must have been difficult for them to part from each other.

"I think I should stay here," I heard Pearl's voice. "It certainly can't hurt to have a secret agent in this house tonight, don't you think?"

Before I could say anything to her, she had already slipped out from under the table and was meowing at

Marlene, who was still sitting on one of the chairs.

The little girl looked at her with a bright smile and immediately did what Pearl—pardon me, Spy 008—had probably intended. Marlene picked up the tiny one, hugged her tightly, and then turned to Victoria in an excited voice.

"Can Pearl stay with me tonight? I think she needs a lot of comfort! She must be terrified, just look!"

I left my place under the table and caught a glance—and a thought—from Pearl. "Terrified ... oh yes! Of the ordeal I'll have to go through to stay here in the house. What kind of shampoo does this little monster use? Her hair smells just awful!"

"Humans don't roll around in fish," I commented, trying to cheer up my brave, self-sacrificing little spy a bit.

I didn't like the fact that Pearl wanted to stay here in the mansion all alone to search for clues during the night. For all we knew, a murderer was living under this very roof.

I would have liked to take on the mission myself, but I couldn't chum up to one of the house's inhabitants in the same way she had. Neither Marlene nor anyone else here seemed to feel the urge to keep *me* with them overnight.

I could tell Victoria was not thrilled with the idea of leaving Pearl with Marlene. But she also didn't have the heart to deny the little girl her fervent wish, not after a man had been shot in the street tonight. So she agreed.

"Oh thank you!" Marlene beamed. "I'll bring Pearl back first thing in the morning then, okay?"

Victoria nodded—and she and I left the mansion to-gether.

19

Pearl did not return.

Neither that night nor the next morning, when Victoria and I were waiting for her at the breakfast table.

No matter how diligently she might have investigated in her role as Spy 008, I couldn't for the life of me imagine what could have caused Pearl to skip her morning serving of salmon.

Victoria ate breakfast without any real appetite, left her part of the salmon untouched, and looked at the clock several times.

"Where is she, Athos? I may be a bad person, but I don't have a good feeling about her being with Marlene. Terrible of me, isn't it? She's a nice little girl, and she's crazy about Pearl."

I took it upon myself to devour Pearl's portion of fish, although I didn't really care for salmon. I only did it in order to tease her later on that I had finally stolen something from her. I really didn't manage to do that very often. Later, when she came stomping through the cat door like a queen, I would needle her with it...

But she did not return. Not even later.

As ten o'clock approached, Victoria didn't want to wait any longer.

"Do you think it would be very rude if I rang the Bruckhausens' bell and brought Pearl back?" she asked me. "It would be fine, wouldn't it? After all, I agreed with Marlene that she would bring Pearl back this morning at the latest. And now it's getting close to lunchtime. Well, almost."

She didn't wait for an answer, but put on a thin vest, ran into the hall, and slipped into the first pair of shoes she found there.

I didn't have to persuade her to take me along. Of course I wanted to help bring the tiny one back.

We walked the short distance over to the Bruck-hausens' mansion without having to use the leash. Victoria called Pearl's name—probably assuming that she was roaming around outside somewhere—while I squinted up at the camera mast where the hawk liked to hang out. He was sitting up there, seemingly taking a nap.

"Have you seen Pearl?" I yelped at him.

Today he actually deigned to answer. He opened one eye. "Pearl?" he asked monosyllabically.

"You know exactly who she is!" I hissed at him. "My cat."

"I don't know," he replied in a bored voice.

I ran as close as I could to the mast and barked at the arrogant bird.

"If you've done anything to the tiny one, I'll pluck out every single one of your feathers!" I threatened him. This at least made him spread his wings and flee the scene.

Victoria hadn't even noticed that I'd stopped—she'd already walked on.

Then, however, she turned to look at me. "What's keeping you, Athos? Now is really not the time to dawdle!"

Erwin opened the door for us after Victoria had maltreated the bell button quite violently.

"Can I help you?" he asked, looking as if we were two ragamuffins who'd dared to ring the bell of a royal mansion.

Victoria pushed past him into the entry hall. "I'm just picking up my cat. She should be home by now."

I also managed to cheat my way past the grumpy valet into the interior of the house. There Victoria called for Pearl, while I tried to pick up the tiny one's trail.

However, I did not succeed—or rather, I found that there were far too many traces of Pearl. She had been here more often lately, and had probably wandered through a large part of the house.

Erwin approached us with a sour face. "Would you please not make such a noise?" he said indignantly. "Whom do you wish to see? Where is your cat supposed to be?"

"With Marlene," Victoria said. "I know where her room is."

Without waiting for an answer from the servant, she hurried up the big staircase and turned left on the first floor. I hurried after her, ignoring the angry sounds Erwin was making.

We did not find Marlene in her room, but ran into

Fabius on the landing. He told Victoria that the little girl was still sitting in the dining room having breakfast with her mother and siblings.

"That's probably what kept Pearl," Victoria exclaimed. "When there's food, she forgets everything else around her."

I couldn't tell if she was talking to Fabius or to me. In any case, the young man took it upon himself to accompany her to the dining room. There was nothing more to be seen of Erwin; apparently he'd given up trying to drive away the troublesome intruders.

In the breakfast room, Amalia, her children and Balduin Bruckhausen were sitting together. The morning meal was already over, judging by the plates that had been duly cleaned. Amalia was typing away on her cell phone, and Balduin was reading a newspaper. The three children were playing on the floor close to their mother.

But there was no trace of Pearl to be seen. Here in this room, it didn't even smell of her. She had clearly not taken part in the breakfast.

Victoria mumbled a few words that sounded like, "Sorry to bother you," then immediately turned to Marlene and asked about Pearl. "You were supposed to bring her back to me this morning," she said, at least managing to put on her friendly therapist face and speak in a calm voice. You had to listen carefully to detect the faint reproach in her words.

Marlene got clumsily to her feet, suddenly making a face as if Victoria had slapped her. The next moment the little girl burst into tears. "I ... when I woke up this morning, Pearl wasn't with me!" she sobbed, "and I can't find her anywhere!"

Amalia jumped up from her chair and ran toward the child. She immediately had a handkerchief in her hand and wiped her daughter's nose.

"Don't cry, dear!" she exclaimed, as if she herself was about to burst into tears at the obvious suffering of her daughter.

It took Victoria a moment to respond. "When did you last see Pearl?" she asked, after Amalia had calmed the child to some extent.

"I took her to bed with me last night," Marlene sniffled. "But this morning she wasn't there. I've been looking all over for her. I thought she'd slipped out of the house and ... run back to you."

Victoria shook her head. "She hasn't."

Balduin folded up his newspaper and looked at his granddaughter in irritation. "Really now, Marlene, you took responsibility for the kitten. Victoria trusted you. And then you just let Pearl run away? You should have taken better care of her!"

Marlene burst into tears again.

"Come on, Dad, is it necessary for you to be so strict?" Amalia turned to her father with a furrowed brow. At the same time, she dug a new handkerchief out of the pocket of her dress and dabbed Marlene's wet face with it.

I'd had enough of the drama. If Pearl was still here in the house, I would find her. Provided that someone opened the doors for me—

I lowered my nose to the floor and walked toward the exit of the dining room. Victoria, fortunately, understood what I was up to.

"Is it all right for my dog to look for Pearl in the house?" she asked, turning to Balduin. "He's probably the best one to track her down."

The old man readily agreed. "Of course; my house is entirely at your disposal. I'm really very sorry that your cat disappeared here, of all places." He gave Marlene another sidelong glance, but this time it was not as stern as the previous one.

I sniffed my way through just about every corridor on the ground floor, and the first and second floor of the mansion. Searching every room was impossible, though. Some of them were locked, and the building was so huge and sprawling that I soon lost my bearings.

Victoria, who was following me and calling for Pearl every few feet, seemed to have gotten lost as well.

When we found ourselves down in the entrance hall once more, after having wandered around for a while, she dropped onto one of the benches that was standing there and took a deep breath.

"It's no use, Athos. Pearl's not here. She would have heard us by now, wouldn't she? And she certainly wouldn't be hiding; that's not like her. She must have slipped out of the house, maybe even during the night. Maybe there was a window open somewhere, since the weather outside has been so mild this time of year."

She lowered her head into her hands and sighed in discouragement.

I ran to her, giving her a gentle nudge with my muzzle. "We'll find Pearl," I said, though I was nowhere near as optimistic as I pretended to be in comforting Victoria.

Where could the tiny one have disappeared to? It really wasn't like Pearl to just vanish. And since she'd moved in with us, I'd at least impressed on her that she wasn't to undertake longer forays outside without my company. She might make fun of her 'Malamute bodyguard' or even complain about it, but she was usually quite happy that I had her back when she was going off on some adventure.

"Where are you, Tiny?" I sent to her in my mind, but I received no answer to that either. We were not whales, who could communicate purely by telepathy with our fellow species members over very long distances. And even those giants of the seas accompanied their thought communication with their songs.

When Pearl sat next to me and consciously sent me a thought, and I could read her expression and body language, it was quite easy to communicate telepathically. Now, however, the kitten and whatever she might be thinking remained hidden from me. It was as if Pearl had been swallowed up by the earth.

Just as Victoria was about to leave the mansion, Balduin appeared in the entrance hall. He didn't have to ask if we had found Pearl in the meantime. One look at Victoria's face was enough for him.

"I'm so sorry," he began.

Victoria put on a brave expression. "We'll find her," she said. "She's probably just hanging around in the gardens somewhere."

The old man nodded and essayed an optimistic smile. Then he said, "Tonight we plan to hold a mourning ceremony here at our house. For Adrian—a dinner, on a small scale. Father Valentin will be with us, and would you perhaps like to join us, too?"

He looked down at me and added, "Of course, your animals are welcome as well. I hope you'll have found your kitten by then."

Victoria accepted the invitation gratefully, but without any real joy. Then we left the Bruckhausens' mansion together.

20

We continued our search for Pearl outside, first walking down the street in front of the houses and then searching in alleys and streets a little further away on our side of the lake.

"Can't you sniff her out?" Victoria asked me. She didn't sound reproachful, only sad.

She was mostly keeping to the sidewalk, but constantly peering into the middle of the street, probably out of the fear of discovering Pearl's flattened body there.

Fortunately we were spared such a sight, but there was simply no fresh trace of the tiny one, no matter how hard I tried to be a perfect tracking hound.

Finally Victoria returned home with me, switched on her computer, and began to create a document with a picture of Pearl on it. Underneath she wrote all kinds of things that I couldn't read, of course, but I assumed it was supposed to be some kind of missing cat notice.

My suspicions were confirmed when she printed out the file dozens of times and then left the house with me again. This time she took me by the leash and walked the streets in our immediate vicinity, attaching the printed notices she had prepared to light poles, fence posts, and alley trees.

I had seen such notices before—it was a common way

people used to look for lost pets. When a two-legged disappeared they did not resort to these posters, but rather called the police.

Again, on this second round through our neighborhood I could not sniff out a trace of Pearl.

When Victoria had hung up all her notes and we were approaching our house again, my eyes fell on the patch of woodland that stretched out behind the Bruckhausen estate. The gunman who had murdered Adrian last night had probably been lurking among the trees that bordered the sidewalk at the end of our street. And it was also this grove that had to be penetrated quite deeply to reach the old forester's lodge where Tim was hiding—if he had returned there at all, and had not long since completely disappeared from our region.

Could it be that Pearl had made her way to the escaped gardener? Had something happened last night in the Bruckhausens' mansion that had prompted the little spy to seek out Tim?

I really couldn't imagine that she wouldn't have stopped by and taken me with her ... but it wasn't impossible. Maybe she had been pressed for time?

I stopped and sat on my hind paws, conflicted about what to do. If I ran into the woods now, dragging Victoria behind me on the leash—if I led her all the way to Tim's lodge, and Pearl was not to be found there—would Tim hate me for revealing his hiding place? Would Victoria hate me for taking her to the man who was possibly a murderer?

"Come on, let's go home," Victoria said to snap me out

of my thoughts. She pulled on my leash to get me to stand up.

I rose, but then I made a quick decision. I simply had to know if Pearl had made her way to Tim. But I needed to go alone.

"Sorry, Victoria," I yelped—and sprinted off.

Fortunately she hadn't been holding my leash too tightly and the thin leather strap escaped her hand without pulling her off her feet. Before she could regain her speech from fright and call something after me, I had already disappeared into the wooded area, between the trees.

Of course she eventually called my name anyway, sounding so insecure, so lost, that it made my heart ache. But she made no attempt to follow me into the forest.

"Did you find a trace of Pearl?" I heard her call out before I got too far away, and her words already sounded a little more hopeful.

I ran as fast as my paws would carry me in the direction of Tim's ruined forest lodge. I had to hurry; I could not leave Victoria alone for too long, couldn't make her fear that now she'd lost me, too. The leash that I was still dragging behind me didn't make running any easier, however. More than once it got between my legs and almost brought me down.

While I was hurrying along, I sniffed for Pearl, of course, but could not pick up her scent trail. Only Tim's faint but unmistakable scent mark clung to the forest floor.

As I approached the half-ruined hut, I abruptly slowed down. An intense scent hit my nose—blood!

I sniffed more intensely, hoping that I was wrong. But the smell was unmistakable. I started running again, following the new trail … and I didn't have to go far.

I found Tim, half stretched out on the forest floor, with his head and shoulders leaning against the trunk of a spruce. It was he who stank so terribly of blood!

His right leg was stuck in a steel trap, a huge metal monstrosity that I knew only from television. I had seen such despicable devices in programs about the far north, which I loved to watch for the sake of my wolfish ancestors: bear traps. Hunters hid them on the forest floor, stretched them open, and when an animal stepped into them, the iron jaws of the murderous instrument would snap shut with full force.

The paw or leg of the unfortunate victim was shredded in the process, the bones crushed … and most of the traps were also anchored into the ground or with a great weight, so that you could not even drag yourself away, even if you might still have been able to do so.

In most cases the trapped victim had no choice but to wait for his end, to bleed to death miserably … if the hunters did not return beforehand and give him the coup de grace.

Tim's leg was stuck in just such a horrific contrivance. How on earth had he gotten into it? What madman had laid a bear trap in our forest?

The ground was soaked with blood and a piece of bone was sticking out of the poor gardener's tattered pants.

He himself was leaning there against the tree as if asleep. For a moment I feared he was no longer alive, but when I approached Tim I felt that he was still breathing, even if only weakly.

His body was cold—not as cold as a corpse would have been, but still very chilled. He had probably been lying here for some time. Maybe since nightfall? Outside on the meadows and on the lakeshore, where the sun's rays were warming the ground, early summer might already have arrived, but here in the eternal semi-darkness of the forest the temperatures were still quite cool … which could be the doom of a creature without fur. Even more so if they were losing blood at the same time.

Tim needed help, and he needed it fast.

21

I sat up straight, put my head back and let out a howl that would have been worthy of a full-grown wolf. "SOS! This human needs help!"

I howled and barked, which at least caused Tim's eyelids to flicker and his arms to move. His fingers stretched and clenched again, but very slowly. However the rest of his body continued to lie there unconscious. His face was scratched and so were his hands, and the hair at the back of his head, only partially visible, seemed to be caked with blood as well.

Whatever has happened to the poor gardener? I asked myself in horror.

At the same time, I realized that my howling was achieving nothing here. I was too far away from the place where I had escaped Victoria, too far from any houses or streets. No one would hear me, and even if they did they would think I was just a stray dog or a wolf making random noise.

I had to get Tim awake. Not just his arms and hands, but the whole man. Maybe he'd have an idea as to how I could help him.

So I did what most people hated, but whereby any dog could practically wake the dead: I stuck my tongue out and slapped it right into Tim's face, several times and with great impetus.

Finally he moaned, reflexively trying to pull his arms in front of his face. I added a little more, drooled all over his ear, nudged him with my muzzle, and barked.

Fortunately, these measures helped. He came to, even though at first he looked at me like a drunk whose eyes couldn't focus properly.

Then, when he'd fully regained consciousness, he groaned in pain. He wanted to pull himself up, feel his leg, which had to hurt like hell, but he couldn't muster the necessary strength to do so. All he managed was to turn his head toward me.

"Athos," he gasped, "good dog..."

Again he moaned, clenching his teeth, and I was afraid that he would soon lose consciousness again from the pain.

But he held on. He was breathing heavily, and had trouble uttering what he wanted to tell me. His lips were cracked and the skin was peeling off in shreds.

"Phone," he finally croaked. He managed to bring his right hand up to his head and press it to his ear, as if he wanted to make a phone call.

"Cell phone ... can you get it for me?" Then he pointed with the same hand in the direction of the ruined forester's lodge, which could be seen—at least partially—between the tree trunks. It was perhaps a hundred paces away, but for him, with a shattered foot, half bled out and caught in a trap from which he could not free himself with the strength he still had left, it was a distance that couldn't be overcome.

I ran off. Fortunately as the house was in ruins I didn't

have to figure out how to get inside.

I found a few scraps of food in the corner of the hut that still had a roof, and in a small pile near the wall there were the few belongings that Tim had taken with him on his escape or had gotten from somewhere in the meantime. A carelessly folded blanket, a crumpled sweater—and the cell phone I was looking for.

I took it carefully between my teeth, pressing my tongue against it because the thing was slippery as hell and I didn't want to drop it on the way, then rushed back to Tim.

He was so pale, as if he were about to turn into a snowman, and his face was still distorted from all the pain he had endured. But he managed a thin smile as I dropped the phone on his stomach.

With shaky fingers, he reached for it, muttered, "Oh, thank God, the battery hasn't died yet," and made an emergency call.

He gave a rough description of his location to the EMT man on duty, then added, "I have a dog with me; I hope he'll bark when he hears you approaching, so you'd best pay attention. That's the quickest way to find me. I don't think I have much time left," he added. "I ... I'm so damn cold. Probably a bad sign."

With that he hung up and let his head sink back against the tree trunk, exhausted.

"Good boy ... Athos," he muttered, "the police will get their hands on me now, of course ... but that's better than dying, I guess." With that, his eyelids closed and he lost consciousness again.

I used the time while waiting for the two-legged help-ers to take a closer look at the spot where Tim was lying. My nose was full of his smell, his blood, but I had to find out what had happened here. So I sniffed around, searching the ground and crisscrossing between the trees, finally running back to the cabin Tim had occu-pied.

I found a scent trail near the hut, and it matched an-other one right where Tim was lying. It belonged to a two-legged who must have been here in the forest to-gether with the gardener. I also knew who the human was, because I recognized the scent—it belonged to Leon, Sabrina's former boyfriend. What on earth had he been doing here in the forest? Had *he* laid the trap that had been Tim's undoing?

I ran back to Tim, and pressed myself against his body to keep him warm. His face was so sunken now that he looked like a dead man. But his heart was still beating, and his breathing was slow but regular. He had a strong constitution. He would hold on until his rescuers ar-rived—hopefully.

I kept watch, my ears pricked, until I heard the sound of a car approaching on one of the forest paths. Then the engine stopped and right after that I perceived the first steps of two-leggeds running through the forest. I once again started my wolf howl and my wild barking, and fortunately I had no trouble luring them to the right place.

When the first paramedic showed up, he stopped short and looked at me fearfully. Did he seriously assume that I would tear him apart just because I was a large dog rather than a cute little kitten?

I ran away from Tim to clear their path. My presence was no longer needed here, anyway. The paramedics would take care of Tim, take him to a hospital, where hopefully they could save his foot.

Meanwhile Victoria was probably worrying herself to death about me. I had been gone for a long time—and my mission to find Pearl at Tim's had failed miserably.

I started to run.

When I scratched at our front door to gain entry, Victoria opened it for me within seconds. She must have run to the door ... and when she saw me, she went down on her knees and pulled me into a bear hug.

"Oh thank God, Athos, you're back!"

She looked outside, probably hoping I had brought Pearl with me, but as far as that was concerned I had to disappoint her.

After squeezing me so tightly that it almost took my breath away, she began to scold me. She didn't sound angry, just scared.

"You can't just run away, Athos!" she reproached. "I was worried sick! Don't ever do that again, okay?"

I licked her hands. "I can't promise," I said, knowing she didn't understand me anyway. "I was just looking for Pearl, after all. And besides, it turned out that Tim needed my help—"

I broke off. How could I explain to her what had

happened to Tim? And that I had smelled Leon's scent there, where the gardener would surely have died if I hadn't found him by chance? She had to know, it could be important, but I had no way to communicate it to her. Once again it drove me crazy that she didn't understand my language.

22

Late in the afternoon, my human received a video call—from Tim. When I recognized his voice, I immediately ran to Victoria to catch a glimpse of her cell phone screen.

He greeted Victoria, sounding uncertain. Shy.

"I thought I should call you," he began. "I'm at the hospital."

Just as I approached Victoria to take a look at Tim, he made his cell phone camera pan across his foot, which was in a thick bandage. "I had surgery," he explained to her. "And I wanted to thank you for Athos—"

He interrupted himself as he let the camera pan back to his face, and spotted me next to Victoria. "Oh, Athos is back with you," he exclaimed. "Thank goodness! I was worried after he just disappeared."

"Wait," Victoria interrupted him. "Athos was with you?"

Tim nodded. "He saved my life, Victoria." He began to describe to her what had happened in the forest: my rescue mission.

The two-leggeds sometimes have the most horrible face colors—from slime-yellow to puke-green—on the screens of their phones and computers, but Tim looked much healthier now than he had earlier in the forest. He was lying in a hospital bed, had tiny band-aids on his face and was managing to smile again.

"I swear, with your animals sometimes one really gets the feeling that they understand every word we say," he told Victoria after filling her in about how I had retrieved his cell phone from the ruined cabin for him.

I lowered my head onto Victoria's thigh in exasperation. "Of course we understand every word," I said to myself. "Unlike you two-leggeds, when *we* try to communicate something to you." Victoria, of course, heard only a yelp, and was unable to understand my complaint.

She stroked my head. "You did a good job, Athos. You're a real hero!" That made me feel a little more conciliated.

Tim continued his report, and Victoria could not believe her ears. "It's just terrible what happened to you!" she exclaimed—more than once.

I smelled, and heard, that she was very grateful for Tim's rescue. She might think he was a murderer, but she was very fond of the man; that was unmistakable.

Finally she asked him the question that had been burning on my own tongue ever since I'd found Tim in the bear trap: "How the hell did you end up in such a monstrous device in our forest? There's no way something like that can just have been lying around. It's been illegal for decades ... hasn't it?"

Tim didn't answer right away. I could see his features darkening, his jaw muscles tightening. "I'm sure that trap wasn't just lying around there by accident. And I didn't step into it myself, either."

"What ... what are you saying?" my human asked breathlessly.

"I was knocked down, Victoria. I woke up during the night in my forest cabin, I don't know why exactly. Maybe I'd heard something, but didn't consciously notice it. Anyway, I went outside, I wanted to ... well, I needed to pee. And that's when I was knocked down from behind."

"Seriously?" asked Victoria. Her voice had died down to a frightened whisper.

"Seriously. I lost consciousness—and when I came to, there was this hellish pain in my leg. I was on the ground, stuck in this iron leghold trap. My foot was shattered and I was bleeding from the wound like I'd been stabbed. I tried to drag myself back to the cabin—it wasn't very far away, I could see it—when it got a little lighter, with daylight dawning. But I just couldn't stop the bleeding, and I kept losing consciousness. The pain was—

"I don't even want to describe it to you, Victoria. By the time your dog found me—I don't know how—I had no hope that I would survive."

"But who attacked you? Couldn't you tell?"

"No. He struck from behind. Or was it a she?—it could have been anyone. I didn't hear them coming, and I didn't have a chance to fight back. I don't even know how they found me."

"Adrian was shot last night," Victoria said after a brief pause. "And the perpetrator was also able to escape unseen."

"I've already heard," Tim said. "The police were here right after my leg was operated on. Inspector Zimmerman told me everything. I swear to you, Victoria, that I had nothing to do with this murder! The inspector seems to believe me. The shot that killed Adrian supposedly came from the forest that borders your street, and where the hut I was hiding in is also located. But the distance in between is several kilometers! I wasn't even near your street! You must believe me, Victoria."

"I do," she said. Her voice still sounded rough and feeble.

"I am being made a scapegoat, again. I didn't kill that McAllister guy and I don't know anything about any drugs I was supposedly going to sell him, which the police accused me of doing. And I certainly had nothing against Adrian. I liked the guy, for crying out loud!"

"If Athos hadn't found you," Victoria said, "your body would have been discovered in the forest at some point. They would have assumed you stepped into that trap during your escape ... but that's madness!" she corrected herself. "Where would you even get a trap like that nowadays? Do they still sell them?"

"Oh, those monstrosities are still lying around in many cellars or old sheds," said Tim. "In our tool shed— that is, at the Bruckhausens'—there are also still such traps, relics from a time when people were not very squeamish. The snares were not only set for animals, but often also for poachers. They perished miserably in them, often under the eyes of the landowners. The nobility didn't take it lightly when people went after their deer. Guido once told me that—our doctor. He still has all kinds of equipment from that time in his cellar."

"That's despicable," Victoria said in a quivering voice.

Tim's words were running through my head. So there were such barbaric contraptions lying around in the doctor's house, and in the Bruckhausens' shed?

The doctor was certainly not the sort of person who was capable of committing murder. He was a very kind human who was only ever concerned with healing people. He wanted to take care of them, to save them from death ... he would not let a man simply bleed to death in the forest. On the other hand, he had been suspiciously quick on the scene last night after Adrian's murder. Was that only because he might have been secretly meeting with Amalia, his beloved, somewhere near the Bruckhausens' mansion? Officially he was no longer welcome there, at least according to Balduin, the patriarch.

I wanted to believe that Guido had not buried his love hopes too quickly and was still secretly seeing Amalia; better that than he was a stone-cold sadistic killer.

And it was not his scent that I had smelled in the forest, but that of Leon. I wouldn't have expected him to commit murder either—but I'd already had painful experiences in the past due to the fact that the two-leggeds were masters of lies and the art of make-believe.

Had Leon grabbed one of the bear traps from the Bruckhausens' shed, followed Tim into the woods and knocked him down there? Only to then smash his leg with this trap and let him bleed to death?

It was bad enough when the oh-so-civilized two-leg-geds slaughtered each other, but to use this method ... it was just atrocious.

Had Leon killed Adrian out of jealousy, because he'd taken Sabrina away from him?

And was Tim right in his assumption that he would be made the scapegoat for Adrian's death, just like before for the murder of Sinclair—which couldn't have anything to do with Sabrina? Or could it?

And how had Leon—if he had actually attacked Tim—found his way into the forest in the first place? To Tim's hiding place in the old forester's lodge?

My skull was beginning to hum horribly in the face of all these questions and complications. How would I ever be able to clear up this mess—without Pearl? That was the question that tormented me most: where was my little midget?

It was the thought of Pearl that led me to find inspiration—for which I would have been puffed up with pride in front of the tiny one, if only she had been with me now.

When I thought of the kitten I saw her favorite enemy, the hawk, in my mind's eye, always perching so stoically on his camera mast. However, it did not occur to me to ask the bird whether he had perhaps observed something that could shed light on the murder cases. No, even if he had, the ill-tempered hawk would certainly not have told me about it.

But it was something else that I now saw in my mind's eye, and that was the hawk's vantage point: the camera that comprised a part of a series of similar surveillance devices belonging to the Bruckhausens. And this one camera, the last one on the front of the property, was oriented to the side in such a way that it overlooked not only the street but also the entrance to our property. Victoria had remarked on that once, shortly after she'd moved in. She hadn't thought it was right that her comings and goings could be monitored in this way by the neighbors.

But Balduin had alleviated her fear. "It's all for our safety, dear Victoria. You can believe me that no one in my family has any interest in spying on you. But cameras are one of the most effective methods of deterring burglars, and that's in your best interest too, isn't it? We just want to monitor as much of the street as we can."

Which meant that Leon might have observed Tim leaving Victoria's house at night, with the help of this camera that stood at the property line. He could have followed him into the forest, and discovered Tim's hiding place there. And he'd been able to return there at any time after that—with the horrible leghold trap, in order to make Tim out to be a murderer who'd suffered a tragic accident on the run. Very bad karma, so to speak.

Maybe Leon had shot Adrian, and then slipped out of the house again that same night to finish Tim off.

A cruel and brilliant plan, but what could I do about it now? How could I convict Leon if he really was the murderer we were looking for?

Victoria's voice snapped me out of my gloomy

thoughts. She was still on the phone with Tim and had meanwhile at least partially regained her composure. "Why did you run away from my house?" she asked him now. "The other night."

Tim suddenly looked sad. "I saw your distrust, Victoria," he said, "after you found out about my criminal record. I couldn't stand to see you afraid of me. So I left."

Victoria said nothing in reply. She only nodded, barely noticeably.

"I didn't want to get you in trouble, either," Tim added. "If I had been found with you and charged with murder, you would have been an accessory. That couldn't be allowed to happen."

"I really wasn't afraid of that," Victoria said.

"I know. You're incredibly brave."

Tim fell silent for a moment. "I shouldn't have lied to you," he said then. "That was stupid of me. But I didn't kill anyone," he affirmed again. "Neither Sinclair nor Adrian. Nor did I have the slightest reason to."

"I believe you," Victoria said. She now seemed genuinely convinced of Tim's innocence. "Will the police arrest you now?" she asked anxiously.

"I hope not. I can't run anyway at the moment, so for now I get to lie in the hospital as a free man. Lucky me," he added with a touch of sarcasm. "And if I'm even luckier, the inspector will believe my testimony about what happened to me in the woods. You see, the police found partial footprints of a second person there. Not only mine, but also my attacker's, although it doesn't look like they can be traced to anyone in particular. They are only partial prints, as I said, and the shoe profile is not a conspicuous one ... but at least it proves that someone else was in the forest besides me. And I think the police also believe me that this trap wasn't just lying around there by accident, or that I would have even hurt myself with it just to prove my innocence. After all, I almost died."

Victoria exhaled audibly. "It's so awful," she whispered. "I'm so glad you're okay."

"Well, I'll be hobbling around like an old dodderer for quite a long time," Tim said, in a tone that almost sounded like the gardener I knew again. Light-hearted, humorous, always ready to make a joke at his own expense rather than poke fun at others.

"But the doctors say I'll be able to walk alright again in the end," he added. "No marathons, maybe—but you won't get a boyfriend with a limp, either." He hesitated for a moment. "That is, if you still want me as a boyfriend, Victoria."

She made no reply, but regarded Tim with a smile that spoke volumes. "I'll visit you at the hospital as soon as I can," she said. "It's just ... I need to find Pearl. She's been missing since last night."

Tim immediately asked what had happened. He seemed to share my and Victoria's concern about the tiny one.

"Oh man, that poor little kitten!" he said sympathetically after hearing all about Pearl's disappearance. "But she's very—how should I put it?—independent. She knows how to hold her own, doesn't she? So let's hope she's just run away, and nothing serious has happened to her. I'd love to help you look for her..."

"Sweet of you," Victoria said, hanging her head dejectedly.

She had infected me with her sadness, and the next moment, before I could do anything about it, my imagination ran away with me. I saw Pearl's tiny body before me ... crushed and bleeding in a bear trap. Had she gotten in the way of the same ruthless two-legged that had almost murdered Tim?

The thought was choking me up.

23

In the evening, when Victoria and I went to the mourning dinner at the Bruckhausens', there was still no trace of Pearl.

The Bruckhausens' cook, an elderly woman whom everyone called Sammy, had outdone herself in dishing up a five-course luxury menu. She had even prepared three courses for me. I was given cold roast beef first, then a piece of steak, and finally ice cream. It would have been heaven on earth if I could have enjoyed the meal, but without the gleeful smacking of the pipsqueak next to me, even the most delicious menu tasted stale.

The two-leggeds at the table were in a similarly subdued mood, remembering the murdered Adrian. Leon was making an effort with Sabrina, who sat there with red eyes and hardly wanted to eat anything.

Amalia also looked as if she'd been crying again. Only her children—Marlene first and foremost—were making a huge fuss. They were playing with dolls and a pull-along car on the floor, but thankfully they kept away from me. They were afraid of me, which was nonsensical, but tonight I was just fine being left alone.

After I had finished my ice cream and people had moved on to drinking coffee and cognac, I decided to look around Leon's room in the mansion. I had already convinced myself at the beginning of dinner that his smell was indeed the one I had detected out in the forest by Tim's cabin. Now I was hopeful that I might find something to use to prove his guilt.

I knew that Leon had been living in the mansion for some time. After all, it had been presumed that he and Sabrina would marry—before Adrian had thwarted that plan. Adrian had also been living in a guest room in the mansion for the past few weeks—should I perhaps take a look around there as well?

I decided that it couldn't hurt, but I wanted to check Leon's room first; after all, I didn't have forever. Victoria was still sitting at the table, drinking an espresso and talking to Sabrina. She didn't even notice me stealing out of the room, but eventually she would become aware of my absence, at the latest when she wanted to return home. So haste was the order of the day.

The room where the dinner had taken place was on the ground floor of the mansion, the Bruckhausens having more than just the one dining room. I walked along the corridor leading to the entrance hall, and tried to pick out Leon's scent traces from those of the other inhabitants of the house. Not an easy task.

I assumed that he lived somewhere on the upper floors, where most of the bedrooms and guest rooms in the mansion were located. It probably made sense to climb the grand staircase first and then search for Leon's trail upstairs in a more concentrated way.

While I was sniffing the various scents of the humans, I was also on the lookout for Pearl again. Her scent was still in one corner or another, clinging to the carpet in the corridor I was walking along. But there was no fresh trace.

There were mostly large common rooms on the mansion's ground floor. There were several dining rooms and salons, a large library, an ancestral art gallery, an armory and a hunting room—and also the utility rooms of the house. The kitchen, for example.

As I ran past it, a hundred delicious smells bombarded my nose. I slowed my run, paused briefly to indulge in the treat—and almost brought Sammy the cook down in the process. She came storming out of the kitchen; the door flew open, and she appeared with a tray on which she was balancing drinks that she probably was going to serve in the dining room. She just managed to stop herself when she saw me. Two steps further and she would have tripped over me. I jumped to the side.

"Hey, Athos, what are you doing here?" she called out in startled but not unkindly fashion. "Shoo, shoo, you have no business in the kitchen!"

I toddled off. The kitchen was not my destination anyway. Sammy disappeared, and I passed another door, behind which there was another seductive smell. It was a rough-hewn wooden door—the door to the basement, I knew. The other day, when I had turned the house upside down looking for Pearl, Maxim Bruckhausen's caring wife Edith had just disappeared through it—and I had spied that beyond it a rough stone staircase led down into the depths. The delicious smell that drifted up to me suggested that—as was usual in people's cellars—there were pantries and storerooms down there.

I was about to walk past the door, but then I paused. The other day I had searched large parts of the house for Pearl, but I hadn't set my sights on the basement. Maybe the little glutton had been attracted by the delicious scents—and was now stuck somewhere down there behind a door that had slammed shut?

Leon was forgotten for the moment; Pearl had priority. Fortunately, the door had a simple handle that you just had to push down. Doorknobs were my nightmare, but this one I got open on the second try.

I ran down the stairs, sniffed, and called softly for Pearl. A single light bulb on the ceiling was switched on ... probably Sammy came down here regularly and had forgotten to turn off the light. It was just fine with me. Compared to the two-leggeds, I saw quite passably in the dark, but not as well as Pearl with her feline eyes. In the complete darkness of a windowless basement room, even she would have had problems.

At the bottom of the stairs I made out several corridors leading in different directions, lined with countless doors. I sniffed, hoping to pick up Pearl's scent trail, but I smelled nothing but various foods. And wine—a smell I didn't particularly like. The Bruckhausens must have had a well-stocked cellar full of it.

Suddenly, it was as if I heard a sound very close to me: the patter of tiny paws. It was coming from a door that was only a few steps away, which was standing ajar. I ran over, and an intense smell of ham and bacon hit me—and of cheese—and of nuts and other nibbles. This was clearly one of the pantries.

I called softly and sent out the thought, "Pearl, are you in there?" The light from the stairway still illuminated the corridor a little, but in the storage room it was pitch dark.

I received no answer. So I crept into the room—and heard it again: the scuffing of tiny paws on the stone floor.

And then I saw it: it was not Pearl, as I had hoped, but a huge, dark brown rat. And I mean really big. It squatted in front of one of the shelves and stared at me with glowing red eyes.

I jerked back, startled, but immediately regained my composure. I was in no danger from a rodent, no matter how imposing it looked.

"Hello," I said, polite as I usually am.

The rat did not seem to feel any fear of me. It ran a few steps towards me, then straightened up on its hind paws and sniffed at me with twitching whiskers.

"I'm looking for a cat," I said. "Tiny, white fur, blue eyes ... have you seen her?"

"Has your dinner escaped you, then?" the rat replied. I could have sworn it was making fun of me.

"I don't want to eat her," I explained. "She's ... my friend. I'm looking for her."

"Strange dog who is friends with a cat," said the rat, "but yes, I have seen her. Here in the house. Upstairs, that is, not down here."

"What? Where? When?" I cried excitedly.

"Hmm. It's been a while. She was with that awful kid. Marlene—"

I couldn't hide my disappointment. "Yes, I know that. But she's been missing ever since."

The rat didn't reply, but I wasn't ready to give up yet.

"You didn't see the cat down here, too, maybe?" I asked.

"No. This is my pantry here, no cats welcome. And neither are dogs, for that matter."

The rodent seemed to me to be a little tired of living. But I couldn't get around to pointing out to him that on the one hand I wasn't interested in his food, and on the other I could have eaten him myself as a second dessert without any problems if I had felt like it.

For at that moment, a cone of light suddenly shone into the room. It belonged to a flashlight in the hand of a two-legged, and in the next moment, the man also turned on the light in the pantry. I recognized him—it was Erwin, the valet.

In his left hand he was holding the flashlight, which he now shone directly into my eyes, blinding me. In his right hand, before I closed my eyelids to avoid the glare, I recognized a broom.

I took a step to the side, blinking.

A diabolical smile was playing on Erwin's face. "Got you, you disgusting creature!" he shouted triumphantly. The next moment he struck. His broom came whizzing down, I made another leap to the side—and only then did I realize that he hadn't been aiming at me at all. He was going for the rat. And the poor thing had not been fast enough to avoid the broom.

It emitted a pained whimper, was hurled with full

force against the shelf, twitched two or three times and then remained motionless on the floor.

Had Erwin, that brutal monster, murdered the poor rodent? The old man was laughing cruelly.

I bared my teeth and growled at him. What a despicable fellow!

But I had underestimated the fiend. I knew that he did not like me, just as he seemed to hate each and every animal with fervor; but never would I have dreamed that he had designs on me as well. Therefore I was not on my guard.

A fatal mistake.

Before I knew what was happening to me, the old man had kicked me, and in the next moment the broom came down on me with full force.

My vision went black.

24

It was cold around me. My fur felt wet—no, completely soaked—and something was pulling me down. An abrupt pain was driven through my nose. A bite.

"Ow, Pearl, you're hurting me," I muttered. "Don't be so rough!"

I heard a voice that definitely did not belong to Pearl. "Wake up, dog! Or do you want to drown?" The sound was so insistent that I finally came to.

Where was I? It was pitch dark, wet, and cold ... and I still had the feeling of falling, into an abyss that had no bottom. I gasped for air—and almost choked! Water! I was in water! Judging by the taste, in our lake. Trapped in a ... sack? Rough material was brushing against my fur, surrounding me on all sides. I couldn't see much, because the water was getting into my eyes, too, and darkness had enveloped me.

I wanted to breathe, needed air ... and recognized the rat from the basement right in front of my nose. It must have been him who had bitten me.

"At last you're awake!" he cried. "I've gnawed an opening! Look, up here, we'll both fit through. But I can't move my legs! The old man broke them with his broom. You've got to help me, dog!"

Swimming ... I had hardly any experience with that, always having limited myself to staying close to the shore where I could still stand on my legs.

I had a feeling that I was about to explode. I needed air! Carefully I opened my mouth, gently grabbed the rat ... and started paddling chaotically with my legs.

I kicked something hard. Stones? Stuffed into the bag with us to make us sink to the bottom of the lake as quickly as possible?

I managed to stick my head into the opening the rodent had created with his teeth. I tore it open wider as I squeezed through, but the sack would not release me. Like a snake it coiled around my legs, pulling me further down. I struggled desperately, having to be careful not to inhale and swallow water again in the process, and at the same time not to mangle the rodent I had wedged between my teeth.

Finally I got rid of the bag, but then new panic overtook me. Which way was up, and which was down? Blackness surrounded me on all sides. I paddled wildly with my paws, and suddenly I heard the rat's voice in my head. He also braced himself against the roof of my mouth, upward. "This way!" he told me, "The direction is right! Paddle! Come on, harder!"

I did as I was told, and finally, we at last broke through the surface of the water.

I let go of the rat, literally spat him out, and gasped for breath. Still the water was pulling me into the depths; it felt as if my weight had doubled. My fur was suddenly as heavy as a stone.

The rodent tried to kick his legs to stay afloat, but his limbs barely obeyed him. It was a miracle that he was still alive at all; the old monster with his broom had badly injured the little one.

I kicked my paws like crazy, reached the rat again in a moment and dipped my head into the water in front of him. When I lifted it up again, I had reached my goal: the rodent was on top of my head, between my ears, where he was safe from drowning.

"Thank you," he squeaked in exasperation.

I myself was not exactly in the best condition. My skull was humming; no, my whole body—the old bastard's kicks and his broom had done a lot of damage to me.

Had that madman actually packed the rodent and me into a sack with a few stones and thrown us into the lake? No doubt on the assumption that this would get rid of us once and for all.

Yes, we were in our lake. The taste of the water had not deceived me. It was dark, the night sky shrouded in clouds, but I could still make out a few outlines. The shore! On the right, the huge Bruckhausen mansion stood, its roof towering over the giant trees of the park. To the left, much smaller and only partially visible because of the vegetation, was the silhouette of Victoria's house. I had to make it all the way there. The distance didn't look terribly far, but the only problem was that I had to cover it by swimming.

I kicked and paddled like crazy, but hardly made any progress.

"Swimming is like running," I heard the rodent say from the top of my head. "Pretend you want to run, and your paws will know what to do."

I tried it, and lo and behold, it worked! At least somewhat. The lake was still pulling at my body as if it wanted to embrace me and drag me to my death, but I managed to keep my snout above water. The weight of the rodent pushed me down, but fortunately, for all his imposing size, he was not so heavy that I couldn't carry him. I ran, or at least imagined that I was running ... and my paws did know what to do. Slowly but surely I approached the shore.

When I reached it, I let the rodent slide into the grass, and shook myself vigorously—as if by doing so I could rid myself not only of all the water but also of the agony I had endured, finally dropping into the grass panting like an old hound.

"Can you walk?" I said to the rodent when I was able to properly breathe again.

He tried to get to his feet, swayed, and fell down again. His two front paws were trembling, but still seemed to be halfway usable. The poor thing's hind legs, however, were just hanging there limply, not moving at all. That was not good at all.

"I'll be fine," said the rodent. "It's not the first time I've gotten in the way of a two-legged. Will just have to rest for a few days—"

Only now did I notice that there was more than just one scar running through his dark brown fur, and that his right ear looked frayed, as if it had been gnawed on. Its tip was completely missing.

"We need to get you to a vet," I said. "I'm sure he'll be able to help you. The two-leggeds are really good at that!"

The rat emitted a grim sound, as if he were laughing bitterly. "A vet? Are you kidding? He'd kill me on the spot, crush me like that old creep just tried to do. As any other two-legged would. Humans don't doctor members of my species, they loathe us!"

Unfortunately the rodent was right about that. The two-leggeds were very selective about which animals were allowed to be their beloved companions, or which were eaten, skinned, plucked—and finally which species were only considered vermin. In the eyes of the humans, they were good for nothing, an absolute nuisance. And rats clearly fell into this last category.

"I'm taking you back to my place," I decided. "There's no way you can stay out here." I couldn't help thinking of the hawk who loved to hunt Pearl. A half-paralyzed rat would certainly make a tasty and easily-earned meal for him.

25

I approached the rodent, gently took him into my mouth again and started moving towards our terrace. When I had covered about half the distance, I heard Victoria's voice. She was running around somewhere in the front of the house, probably out on the street, calling for me.

She sounded panic-stricken. Obviously she had not been able to find me again in the Bruckhausen mansion, and Erwin, the old monster, had certainly not let on by a single word or look that he had knocked me down and tried to drown me in the lake.

The old monster will be quite surprised when I show up alive, went through my head. And then I will sink my teeth into his behind....

That's as far as I got with my fervent thoughts of revenge.

"Ow, don't squeeze so hard!" I heard the rodent's pleading call between my teeth.

"Sorry!" I hastily replied.

Again Victoria called my name, sounding even more desperate now.

I quickly covered the last few steps to the terrace, where I set the rodent down right in front of Pearl's cat door.

"I'm going to push you through there, okay?" I said to

the rat. "You just stay where you land and I'll come get you as soon as I can make it inside. I can't fit through here ... and besides, I have to take care of my human."

"All right," said the rat. I carefully pushed him through Pearl's door with my snout and he remained lying there right behind it. He seemed to be in excruciating pain, but was acting very brave.

I hurried off in the direction of the street and began to bark loudly. I had no trouble getting Victoria's attention.

She came running towards me, pushed open the garden gate, probably aiming to scold and hug me again at the same time, because in her eyes I had escaped once more—but then she stopped abruptly. "Good heavens, Athos, what a sight you are!"

While she was taking me into the house, she was already calling our vet on her cell phone. "An emergency," she explained to the man, who had apparently already been asleep. Anyway, from what I could hear of his voice he sounded very dazed at first.

But then, when he had composed himself and Victoria described to him in terse words that I was "badly hurt," he promised to come to us as soon as possible.

And he kept his word: I was brought into the living room, placed on a blanket on the floor, and thoroughly scrutinized by both Victoria and the vet. I knew that behind the sofa, which stood in front of the terrace doors, there lay the poor rodent I had smuggled in through Pearl's catflap. Fortunately the couch was blocking the two-leggeds' view of that spot.

I knew that the brave rodent who had saved us from a watery grave needed the vet's attention much more than I did. But I also knew not to draw the humans' attention to my fellow sufferer; it would have meant his certain death.

After the vet had examined me thoroughly, he began cleaning my wounds and smearing a smelly tincture on them.

To Victoria he said, "From the looks of it, your dog has been badly beaten up. Someone must have kicked him or hit him with a hard object. Maybe both." The doctor shook his head in horror. "But he'll be fine, I think. There's nothing broken, no organs injured, as far as I can see..."

"Who the hell did this?" Victoria cried, furious. "If I get my hands on him—"

The doctor patted my neck sympathetically while nodding to Victoria at the same time.

"But what I don't understand," she continued, "is why Athos is so soaking wet—surely he didn't go swimming after he was attacked? He's not usually a water lover at all, you know."

The doctor shrugged. "I really don't know what happened there, Dr. Adler."

He began to put a bandage on me. I bravely held still, and when he'd finally finished he rose to his feet. "I'll come back tomorrow and check on my patient, okay?"

"Yes, please," Victoria said, then effusively thanked the doctor for being available so quickly and at such a late hour.

He dismissed it with a casual wave of his hand. "Really, that goes without saying. That's what I'm here for, after all."

Victoria set out a bowl of cold chicken for me, leftovers from one of her meals, then disappeared into the bathroom.

I temporarily left the food untouched, waited until Victoria had gone to bed, then limped back into the living room. The pain in my body had become more intense since the doctor had treated me. But it wasn't my condition that I was worried about. I found the rodent where I had left him, by Pearl's cat door behind the sofa.

First we exchanged some wordless glances, sniffing each other, then the rat said, "Thanks for your help, dog. You're a good chap."

"My name is Athos, by the way," I replied.

"Three-tooth," the rodent introduced himself.

Before I could ask him how he'd gotten this unusual name, he opened his muzzle demonstratively and bared his fangs. Where two of his lower razor-sharp front teeth should have been, only one protruded. The other one was broken off. The teeth in the upper jaw, however, were intact.

The rat's whiskers vibrated. "I can still gnaw pretty darn well in spite of everything, don't you think?" he said.

"Damn good!" I confirmed.

Then I asked him if he was hungry and brought him a few pieces of chicken from my food bowl. After that, I got a snout full of water for him to imbibe, but that rather escalated into a shower for the poor guy.

"Thank you, but I'm not thirsty," he said politely. "I've truly had enough water for today."

I looked around, searching for a safe place for my new house guest. I had no idea whether he would ever be able to walk again, even though he was a fierce and robust little guy. Well, actually a very big guy, for his kind. In any case, Victoria could not be allowed to see him.

"What do you say we hide you right here, under the sofa," I suggested. The gap between the piece of furniture and the floor was wide enough to accommodate him. And under the sofa he could rip out some of the upholstery with his sharp teeth and make a comfortable bed for himself.

The suggestion met with Three-tooth's favor. He tried to get onto his feet, was able to crawl a bit forwards on his front paws, but then needed a gentle push from me to disappear completely under the sofa.

I was—quite literally—dog-tired, and wanted to curl up for a nap right there and then. I decided to stay close to my patient, even though I was far from being able to help him as well as the vet would have done.

Before I could surrender to sleep, though, I heard Three-tooth's voice: "That cat you were looking for in my pantry ... she lives here with you?"

"Yes, her name is Pearl. And I can't find her anywhere."

"She's your friend, even though she's a cat?"

"That's right," I said.

"Hmm. I'll help you track her down," said Three-tooth.

"Even though I'm not much good for anything myself right now, my kind—my friends—will look for your kitten. And if she's still alive, we'll find her. I promise."

"That's nice of you," I said, with a lump in my throat. *If she's still alive* ... the words hurt more than the kicking from the old creep who had tried to murder me.

"Last time you saw her—it was in our mansion?" Three-tooth continued.

"Yes, she was with the little girl. Marlene."

"Ghastly child," said Three-tooth. "Then that's where we'll start our search."

"But isn't that dangerous?" I objected. "If you get in the way of that crazy valet—"

"Pah," said Three-tooth. "My family and I, we've lived in the mansion for generations. We know how to avoid the madman. We walk on paths that are completely invisible to him and his kind. I was just a little distracted tonight ... because a giant dog suddenly appeared in my pantry. Otherwise, the creep would never have caught me!"

"I'm sorry," I muttered.

"That's all right; he probably couldn't have knocked you out either if you hadn't just met the most imposing rat of your life."

I found it amazing that the rodent was still capable of humor, in view of his battered condition and the pain that surely tormented him. And somehow his overconfidence reminded me of my midget.

"Do you think that disgusting valet might have gotten Pearl too?" I voiced the thought that had suddenly come over me like a dark cloud.

Three-tooth did not spare me. "It's possible, I'm afraid," he said. "But if he killed her and left even the slightest trace in the process, we will find it. And then you can maul him, and we'll make a feast out of him for my entire clan!"

I really am a peace-loving dog in general, but I must admit that the thought filled me with grim satisfaction. It was definitely better than imagining Pearl, beaten to death and lying in a bag of rocks at the bottom of the lake.

The kitten also had sharp teeth. She, too, could have gotten out of a sack, though perhaps not with the precision and speed of the rat. But Pearl was not a good swimmer, more of a sofa cat than an expert in the great outdoors....

Oh Tiny, what has happened to you?

26

Early the next morning Victoria left the house to visit Tim in the hospital. I was not allowed to go with her.

"You have to get well first, Athos," Victoria said, not entering into a discussion with me this time. To be honest, I didn't mind staying at home. Three-tooth wanted to organize his rat friends to look for Pearl.

"And I need your help with that, Athos," he'd explained. "You're my doorman, okay?"

"Your what?"

"You need to open the door through which you brought me into the house yesterday—your catflap. Then I can call for my family and friends. I myself..." He cheeped in frustration. "I'm not yet back on my paws again."

He peeked out from under the sofa, looking at me with his dark beady eyes, trying to move his legs. His hind paws barely managed more than a twitch.

"Come on, let's get started," he said.

So I ran to Pearl's door, which was designed to open automatically when you approached it. An impressive example of what humans call *technology*.

I placed one of my paws in front of the door to hold it open, lowered my muzzle, which just barely fit into the small opening, and called outside, "Hello, friends and family of Three-tooth, the rat! He's here with me, he's—

" I hesitated, then opted stout-heartedly for: "he's doing quite well," which was perhaps a bit optimistic. "He, that is we, need your help please!"

Three-tooth joined me with a loud squeaking. I heard names, orders, calls … and soon had the impression that I was looking at a field marshal in rat fur.

"Let's hope some of your friends are around at the moment and are able to hear us," I said.

Three-tooth looked at me as if I were a bit feebleminded. "You haven't had much business with rats before, have you?"

I had to admit that he was right.

"We are everywhere," he explained to me. "The world humans believe to be theirs is really ours, you'll see. Several rats will have heard us, and they will pass on the message. Soon they will all come."

He turned his head. "As for finding your cat, we will have my friends pick up Pearl's scent trail. That'll make things easier. Where's the strongest smell your friend has left around here?"

I didn't have to think about it for long. The armchair, which was right next to the sofa, was one of Pearl's favorite spots in the whole house. It smelled intensely of her.

I was amused, however, by the idea that rats were able to follow scent trails like dogs can. I knew, of course, that cats were capable of doing this, but they were not experts at tracking compared to us. And I had honestly never thought about the olfactory abilities of rats.

I was probably musing a little too loudly, because

Three-tooth suddenly said, "You don't think we're as good at sniffing as you are? You've got that wrong, buddy! Our noses are even better than yours, so much so that word has actually spread to the two-leggeds. We help them sniff out explosives—or germs. We are super specialists among sleuths, so to speak! Sniffing out a cat is a cinch!"

I fervently hoped that he was right, and that his friends would succeed in tracking down Pearl.

Three-tooth had told the truth about the widespread distribution of his species. Our call for help was heard, and Three-tooth's fellow rats didn't take long in coming. Before I knew what was happening, the first rat was scurrying in through the cat door. Then the next. Soon they were arriving in twos and threes, and in no time there was a traffic jam outside Pearl's catflap. And they also came into our house by other means, into our living room, suggesting that some of them had been living under our roof even though I had never noticed them.

Three-tooth seemed to be a respected leader in the rat community. He gave out marching orders that were not questioned by any of the other animals. He sent out hordes of rats into the surrounding area, more hordes into the Bruckhausens' mansion, and also into other buildings in the neighborhood. The lakeshore was tackled, as well as the gardens and the wooded area that bordered our settlement.

Many of the rats that came and went bore scars as obvious as Three-tooth's himself on their small, muscular bodies. Some had a mutilated tail, a half-bitten ear, and one was even walking on just three paws. You could tell they were not the cherished favorites of the two-leggeds, receiving the best medical care.

I tried to imagine how it must feel not to have a human, and I felt sorry for the little rodents at the thought. Humans could be hideous, like Erwin the valet; but they could also be smart, lovable, and just wonderful, like Victoria or my late professor.

Certainly Three-tooth's friends were not outspoken fans of cats, but each of them was immediately ready to go in search of my missing pipsqueak. This mission was certainly not an everyday occurrence in the rodent world.

At some point during the morning, while the rats were still going in and out, it began to rain. As a result there was soon a muddy trail of tiny pawprints stretching from the cat door all the way to the seat of the fauteuil, where the rodents had picked up Pearl's scent. How in the world was I going to explain this to Victoria when she returned?

Finally, a rather small brown rat appeared, who was greeted especially warmly by Three-tooth ... and who seemed to be very concerned over his ailing condition.

"Let me introduce you," Three-tooth addressed me. "This is one of my youngest sons, Rémy."

The little rodent looked at me rather shyly. Probably he had never come so close to a big dog like me.

"Rémy?" I repeated. "But that's..."

"Yep! The rat from *Ratatouille,* the famous human animated movie," the little one confirmed with a proudly swelling chest. "The one who can cook so well that he is allowed to run a luxury restaurant of the humans. I want to follow a similar path, so I appropriated the name. I just have to convince our cook, Sammy, to hire me as an assistant!"

"The Bruckhausens' cook?" I asked incredulously.

"Yeah, right. She's not quite the rat lover, you know. At least not yet."

I saw Three-tooth's whiskers vibrate in amusement at his son's words. "The youth of today, Athos!" He sighed theatrically. "They're full of the craziest ambitions! And I always say that human television corrupts good character. But of course no self-respecting young rat listens to his old dad—isn't that right, Junior?"

Rémy twitched his nose a little sheepishly, and then Three-tooth assigned him to look for Pearl's tracks in the Bruckhausens' kitchen. "After all, you know your way around there, don't you?" Three-tooth said.

The little one scurried over to Pearl's fauteuil like his peers before him, climbed up nimbly and sniffed around on the seat like the best-trained police search dog.

"We'll find your friend, buddy," Rémy said to me, already considerably more nonchalant than when he'd arrived. He seemed to have overcome his fear of big dogs remarkably fast. "And hopefully you'll get back on your paws soon, Pop!" he added, addressing Three-tooth in a worried tone.

The big rat assured the younger that he was indestructible, and in the best paws with me as far as his recovery was concerned. He beamed with fatherly pride when the little one took his leave again, and I suddenly had a vision of a little rat with a chef's hat on his head in front of my mind's eye.

I shook myself to get rid of the ludicrous image; the television of the two-leggeds could truly make one a little crazy in the head.

When Three-tooth and I were finally on our own again, I served him some treats that I had managed to scrounge out of the kitchen, mostly because they'd been lying around freely. I wanted to be deserving of his praise that he was in the best paws with me.

After he had eaten with a fairly healthy appetite, he said to me: "You must have a little patience now, Athos. We cannot walk through people's houses or gardens in broad daylight as you do. As I said, we have our own secret ways. So the search may take some time. But if your cat is still alive, we will find her. Upon my honor as a rat!"

When Victoria finally returned home, I had some explaining to do. I received her in the hall, where she hugged me more warmly than she usually did in greeting.

"Sorry I was gone so long, Athos," she said with a rather guilty expression. "I was driving around the neighborhood for a while after my visit with Tim at the hospital. Quite a long time in fact ... but no sign of Pearl, I'm afraid. Where on earth could she be, Athos?" She gave me another hug, this time an even tighter one.

Then her face brightened, at least a little. "Tim is on the mend," she explained to me. "And it looks like he's not going to be arrested, after all." She took a deep breath. "That's a bright spot, at least."

When she finally entered the living room and discovered the muddy trail of countless paws leading to Pearl's fauteuil, she let out a sharp scream. It was a joyful cry, because at first she thought that Pearl had returned home. But immediately she realized that the paw prints were far too small to have been made by a cat—and far too numerous.

"Oh my goodness, what happened here?" she cried.

In the next moment she sucked in air through her nose, as if she wanted to try her hand at being a sniffer, too. Probably the wet-rat aroma that was still lingering in the room was so intense that even the almost odor-blind human nose could detect it.

I tried my best to look completely innocent and immediately fled the scene.

Victoria continued her soliloquy a bit further, but would never have guessed in a hundred years how the marks had actually been made and for what reason.

In the end she fetched the mop and some rags from the storeroom, and set about cleaning the armchair and the floor. She stopped in front of the cat door, where the trail clearly led, and stared out into the open. I peered in from the hall, but didn't make my presence known. Eventually Victoria wiped the last section of floor clean and that was the end of the matter. I breathed a sigh of relief.

As she left the storeroom again, I yelped at her and ran to the coat rack where my leash was hanging. This was a call that I had already trained Victoria to understand well. She knew what I wanted: to go *walkies*, as she put it. She reached for the leash—but stopped immediately. Out of habit she had reached for the double leash that she used to walk Pearl and me together.

With a sad look on her face, she hung it back on the coat rack and took the single leash instead—which dated back to the time before Pearl had moved in with us.

On the one hand I actually felt the need to stretch my paws a bit outside, but I also had a very specific goal: the Bruckhausens' mansion, where I wanted to finally take a look around Leon's room. I didn't yet have a plan for how I was going to make it in there, but once outside on the street, I pulled Victoria in the right direction: over to our neighbors.

"What's wrong, Athos?" she asked me. "Where are you going?" She had realized by now at least that there was a good reason when I pulled too hard on the leash, steering her in a certain direction.

I ran ahead of her, over to the Bruckhausens, and she followed me. While I trotted along I racked my brains for a way to convict Leon. How could I make Victoria, or any other human for that matter, understand that he had been with Tim in the woods? That the footprints the police had found there had to come from him?

Should I lead Victoria to the man's shoes, if they

happened to be standing around somewhere, freely accessible to anyone? Would she understand? Probably not.

Would Leon possibly realize before my human did that I was on to him? Was I risking my neck and putting Victoria in danger?

What a bummer. It was not a good plan. But I couldn't think of a better one; if the tiny one had been with me, I could have discussed it with her here. I had always been sure that I was the better sleuth of the two of us, but now ... I missed her.

I didn't pull on the leash any further, and when we reached the entrance to the Bruckhausens' mansion I trotted past it as if nothing had happened. In the end, it became—at least for Victoria—just an ordinary walk with her dog.

I gave up my plan to lead Victoria to Leon for the time being. I didn't want to endanger her, and frankly at this point I almost didn't care if Leon were guilty, whether he or someone else had killed Sinclair and Adrian, and for what reason. Let the crazy two-leggeds kill each other. Why should I care?

The important thing was that Tim was no longer in danger from the police. That goal seemed to have been achieved. Victoria would get him back as soon as he was allowed to leave the hospital.

I, on the other hand—would I ever get Pearl back? The rats were my last hope.

27

The next morning we were awakened by police sirens. Driven by curiosity, Victoria jumped out of bed, quickly put on a robe and hurried into the hall. She yanked open the front door and peeked out.

I squeezed through past her legs and ran a few steps towards the garden gate.

The police cars with their wailing sirens were parked on the driveway of the mansion. Several policemen were running around—and one of them at last had the idea to turn off the droning sirens after all. People came rushing out of the mansion.

"Come Athos, let's go see what happened," I heard Victoria's voice behind me.

I ran back toward her. She had pulled a vest over her robe, slipped into sneakers and now put on my leash. I trotted over to the Bruckhausens at her side.

We had not yet reached the gathering of people when Sabrina spotted us and came running toward us; tears were streaming down her face. She threw herself into Victoria's arms and buried her face in the crook of my human's neck.

"Leon," she sobbed, heartbroken. "He's dead!"

I saw Victoria stiffen. "Dead?" she repeated in a toneless voice.

"We found him this morning," Sabrina reported

haltingly. She broke away from Victoria, and tried to wipe the tears from her eyes with the back of her hand. But new ones immediately started pouring out.

"I found him myself," she said then. "In his bed, with a syringe next to him, like he was a junkie!"

"Drugs?" Victoria exclaimed. "Oh, God, I didn't know he was—"

"That he was an addict, you mean?" Sabrina sniffed. "He wasn't! I'll never believe that!"

"Come on, dear, let's sit down somewhere," Victoria suggested. "Perhaps Erwin can bring you a cup of tea." She looked around for the beastly house servant, but there was no sign of him.

Balduin Bruckhausen was standing in the driveway talking to the police officers. Other family members had gathered around him. I recognized Maxim, Edith and Amalia.

Thanks to my good ears, I caught a few words from the patriarch: "...our family ... haunted by death ... what have we done to deserve this?"

I couldn't believe it. Another dead human? That was impossible. And Leon, my prime suspect, of all people?

I followed Victoria, who took Sabrina into the Bruckhausens' park and sat down with her on one of the sofas under the plane tree. There was no tea, because Erwin hadn't shown up, but still my human managed to calm Sabrina down a little. Eventually no more tears came, and the young woman seemed to fall into a kind of trance. "Now I've lost them both," she muttered to herself. "I must be cursed..."

A little while later, Maxim and Edith joined us, as did their son Fabius. They all looked as if they had walked through the realm of the dead themselves. They tried hard to comfort Sabrina, hugged her, handed her handkerchiefs when she began to sob again, and spoke to her in low, muffled voices.

At some point Balduin showed up and suggested that we move to the larger terrace so that everyone would have room and could mourn together, as he put it. Amalia brought her children, and eventually even Erwin joined us. Balduin sent him to fetch tea and cake for everyone.

The valet gave me a look as if he had encountered a ghost.

I growled softly. "Quite a surprise, hmm, you monster? You didn't succeed in murdering me. Or Three-tooth either!"

He muttered something to himself that sounded like "disgusting, these dirty animals." Then he disappeared into the house before I lost my temper and sank my teeth into his rear end.

We spent almost the whole day on the terrace. Or, that is, the humans did. They were sitting there as if they had completely lost control of their limbs. They spoke little, drank plenty of tea, but hardly ate any of the cake or sandwiches that Erwin served after lunchtime.

Balduin tried to at least get Sabrina to eat. When that didn't work, he sent for hot chocolate, which she eventually started to sip a little. Victoria also stayed by her side and tried to comfort her.

I wandered aimlessly around the garden, but did not leave the immediate vicinity of the two-leggeds. I kept a lookout for Three-tooth's fellow rodents, found one or another spot where it smelled of rat, but didn't see a single one of them.

When I returned to the terrace, Father Valentin had just arrived. He was given a reasonably warm welcome, was also served tea and cake—and helped himself with a bigger appetite than the family members.

A little while later he invited everyone to pray together. Some of those present folded their hands, others bowed their heads, while Sabrina stared out at the lake. The priest said several prayers, first for the dead, then for the living, and finally he took his leave again.

A little while later, when the day was almost coming to an end, Balduin called Inspector Zimmermann. He summoned him as if he were another of his servants— and the inspector did indeed turn up in the garden obediently. Apparently Balduin and he had known each other within the community for a long time, and Zimmermann seemed to have great respect for the head of the Bruckhausen family.

With an erratic gesture, and a sideways glance at Sabrina, Balduin offered the policeman a seat at the table. The inspector was also waited upon by Erwin, although the valet seemed to dislike policemen just as much as pets. He served the man only with extreme reluctance, looking as if he had bitten into a lemon.

Balduin asked Zimmermann about the latest stage of the investigation. "What actually happened to Leon?" he wanted to know. "Did he really inject himself with an overdose?"

"We don't have any official results yet," the police officer replied, "it's too early for that, I'm afraid."

But Balduin did not let that stand. "Official results!" he snapped. "What the hell does that mean? We don't need a frigging press release. We want to know where you stand—or your colleagues in the CID."

"I really can't—" the inspector began, but Balduin cut him off again.

"Let us hear *your* opinion, man!" the patriarch demanded. "You're allowed to express it, aren't you? What happened to Leon? What does it look like? You are an experienced policeman, aren't you? You will be able to judge the facts of the case as they stand, I take it."

Zimmermann put on a grim face, but at the same time he seemed to realize that Balduin would not rest until he got his way.

The policeman took a sip of tea, then cleared his throat and began to report: "Well, if we go by the initial findings of the coroner and our forensics team ... it appears that Leon Kastner's cause of death was indeed an overdose," he said. "Heroin—and it looks like he injected it on purpose. He also took a strong dose of sleeping pills beforehand. So he wanted to die, I should think."

"Leon certainly didn't commit suicide!" Sabrina cried. "I'll never believe that. He would never have done that to me."

"You spurned him,"—Amalia suddenly took the floor—"have you forgotten? You wanted to marry Adrian!"

Not very tactful; Balduin gave her a stern look, but did not interfere.

Sabrina blinked. "But I ... still loved Leon," she whispered, her lips barely moving as she spoke. Probably only I could hear her words.

The inspector cleared his throat again. He certainly had no desire to get involved in a family discussion at this point. "There could be another reason for Mr. Kastner's suicide," he began cautiously. "Perhaps it was his conscience that drove him to his death. Or the fear that we would soon expose and arrest him..."

All eyes were now fixed on the policeman.

"The fact is," he continued, "that we were able to match the footprints we discovered in the woods where Tim Mortensen was attacked to shoes belonging to Mr. Kastner. The results came in just as you called me earlier."

Now it was Balduin who flared up. "You mean to say Leon did this to Tim? That bear trap?"

"It looks like it, yes," the inspector said. "As I mentioned, these are only preliminary results that I shouldn't even be telling you about yet—"

Balduin made an impatient hand gesture that silenced the inspector. But the old man himself did not speak any further. His eyelids were flickering as if he might lose consciousness at any moment.

"You mustn't get upset, Papa," said Maxim, who himself was sitting there so lopsided and limp that he might have toppled off his chair at any moment.

Balduin took a deep breath, or rather he tried to. It sounded more like a tortured gasp.

The pain, the fear, the confusion of the two-leggeds was making them emit a cocktail of intense scents that burned my nose. Nevertheless, I stayed where I was; I was eager to find out if the police inspector had anything more to report.

But that was not the case. He only elaborated a bit more on what he had already hinted at—namely, that the police not only classified Leon's death as a suicide, but that they now saw in him the murderer of Adrian and Sinclair. And the attack on Tim was also blamed on Leon.

"The gardener was to be made the scapegoat," Zimmermann proclaimed.

"And the motive?" Victoria now took over the conversation. "Why should Leon have committed all these bloody deeds?"

"Well, pathological jealousy, I suppose," said the inspector. "Apparently he not only saw Adrian Seeberg as a competitor, as far as Miss Sabrina was concerned, but possibly the other men—Mr. McAllister and Mr. Mortensen—too. Maybe that's why he tried to pin his crimes on the latter. And when that failed, he tried to kill him as well, trying to make it look as if Mr. Mortensen had escaped and died in a tragic bear trap accident."

Zimmermann paused for a moment, then added: "As

for Mr. Kastner's actual motives, we might never learn the whole truth. He did not leave a suicide note explaining himself to us."

"I'll never believe that story about Leon's suicide," Victoria said to me when we had finally returned to our house. "It doesn't fit at all. He wasn't the kind of person who would leave life voluntarily, or who was prone to delusional jealousy. No, Athos, I really can't imagine that. There's something fishy about this!"

28

Later, when Victoria called Tim at the hospital via video chat, she reiterated the concerns that she had expressed to me.

"This policeman's theory doesn't make any sense at all!" she insisted. "That Leon should have been jealous of Adrian—agreed. But of Sinclair McAllister? I don't recall Sinclair ever exchanging so much as a single word with Sabrina. He certainly wasn't interested in her, nor she in him. Sinclair was murdered because he was snooping around in my father's archives, and found a notebook, which he stole. It must have contained something that could be very dangerous to someone ... and that's why this person was willing to kill for it."

"I think Sinclair's murder was about the Bruckhausens' treasure," Tim said. "Maybe there was something in the notebook that your father found out about it—possibly even the location of the treasure stash?"

Tim was sitting upright in his hospital bed; his facial scratches were healing nicely.

Victoria, on the other hand, was lying on the sofa in the living room and balancing her laptop, which she was using for the video call this time, on her thighs. Of course she didn't have the slightest idea that there was another sickbed under the sofa, one floor below so to speak.

I squinted into the dark crack and could make out Three-tooth's shape there, but the rat seemed to be taking a siesta.

Victoria nodded vigorously. "And my father may also have been..."

She broke off.

Tim said, "We don't know if he was murdered, too, Victoria. I know I've expressed concerns about his death myself, but we don't have any real proof that anything was actually done to him."

"We have no evidence anyway," Victoria said, groaning softly, "for any of our theories. But Leon ... I could swear he didn't inject himself with that overdose. It just doesn't fit his personality."

"Didn't you say they also found an anesthetic in his body?" said Tim. "Maybe that was administered to him by someone without his knowledge. Mixed into a drink—a dish?—and that person then later crept into Leon's bedroom and gave him the lethal injection, without him noticing or even being able to defend himself, because he was fast asleep."

"It must have played out like that, or in a very similar fashion," Victoria said. "Which means the murderer is still on the loose, and will possibly kill again. But on the other hand, I don't understand what Adrian or Leon could have had to do with the Bruckhausens' treasure. Were they not murdered by the same person as Sinclair McAllister, or are we simply dealing with a crazed killer who has no comprehensible motive at all? Is he a psychopath who kills people at random simply because he finds pleasure in murder? Not that I'm a criminal psychologist..."

"Seems to me the role suits you just fine," Tim said with a grim smile. "Maybe you should reorient yourself professionally."

Victoria did not respond to his suggestion. "What are we going to do now, Tim? I can't run to the police and present some abstruse theories. *Inspector, the sequence of events doesn't seem conclusive to me.* That would make me look ridiculous, wouldn't it?"

"Probably," Tim said.

Then, however, his face lit up all at once. "There's something I've been meaning to tell you, Victoria. I found something out!"

"About the murders?"

Tim's brow furrowed. "No ... well, maybe indirectly. Remember that woman who was so beloved of Artur Bruckhausen, whom your father mentioned in his notes? Her strange pet name, Hathor ... I did some research and found out who that was!"

"An Egyptian goddess," Victoria said. "Similar to the Roman Venus or the Greek Aphrodite."

"But—how do you know?" Tim looked disappointed.

"Sabrina told me. She's a budding historian, after all, and she could do something with the name."

"Yeah, huh, I see ... but there's something I'm sure she couldn't tell you," Tim continued with a renewed note of triumph in his voice. "I mentioned the other day that the name sounded familiar to me, didn't I? And when I found out that Hathor was a goddess, that's when I remembered *how* I knew the name."

"Oh yeah—where from?" Victoria leaned forward, as if she wanted to climb into her computer screen.

"From the Bruckhausens' park," Tim said, now smiling broadly and victoriously. "And not from the garden I tend, but from the overgrown part. Hardly anyone strays there these days, it's almost a jungle ... but I undertake a little expedition now and then. I like it in there very much."

Me too, I added to myself.

"And that's where you came across the name of Hathor?" Victoria asked incredulously.

"Not just the name," Tim said, "but a statue of the goddess. It is badly weathered, and the inscription on its pedestal is barely decipherable. But it does read *Hathor*."

"A statue of a goddess in that jungle?" said Victoria.

"Well, at some point this was also part of the Bruckhausens' park, a natural English garden in the Romantic style. At that time, people loved artificial grottoes, and buildings that were already erected as ruins. Small chapels, pagan temples and the like ... follies. The ultra-rich even had original ruins brought to them, which were removed from countries like Greece and then reassembled stone by stone in the park at home. And mythological figures were also very popular, so in the Bruckhausens' park you can find all kinds of gods and heroes. Hathor fits in there very well."

"But at the same time, it was a kind of pet name that Artur Bruckhausen gave to his childhood sweetheart,"

Victoria said.

"His childhood sweetheart?" Tim repeated. "Not his mistress with whom he had an affair?"

"No affair. He knew Käthe long before he met his future wife; I also learned that from Sabrina. He must have been very much in love with this woman, but she passed away."

"She was Artur's 'greatest treasure,'" Tim quoted. "Your father wrote that down several times. Don't you think that this statue of Hathor might give a clue to Artur's other treasure? The one comprising the gold and jewels that he tried to hide decades after the death of his childhood sweetheart?"

"Wow—yes, there's something to that idea!" Victoria exclaimed. "Back when Artur wanted to support the Nazis, that is, shortly before his unexpected death, the garden was already overgrown. Surely that wouldn't be the worst place to hide something of great value. Such a jungle..."

"I think so, too," Tim affirmed.

He panned the cell phone camera to his plastered leg. "When I'm able to walk again, we really need to take a look around near this statue of Hathor. It's been a while since I last saw her, but I hope I can still find my way there. I would ask you to take a look on your own in the meantime, but you would get hopelessly lost. I'm afraid I can't give you any useful directions..."

"That's all right," Victoria said quickly.

I could tell she had little desire to go on a wilderness expedition on her own.

"If Hathor really can lead us to the treasure," she added, "it will still be there in a few weeks, when you can walk again."

Tim replied something, but I didn't catch it, because at that moment Rémy came rushing in through the cat door.

"We've got her!" he squealed, so excitedly—and so loudly—that even Victoria could hear him. She jumped up from the sofa, almost knocking her laptop to the floor, and whirled around.

I just managed to shove Rémy under the sofa with my muzzle before Victoria's gaze fell on him.

"What was that?" she cried, half panicked. "Oh God, Athos, that sounded like a rat! Or am I losing my mind as well?"

She swayed on her legs, looking around with an anxious expression.

"What's wrong?" Tim's voice came from the laptop my human had carelessly dropped on the sofa. "Victoria? Is everything all right there?"

"I ... heard a rat," she called out, loud enough for the laptop to transmit her words. "Or maybe a mouse, I'm not sure. Anyway, it was a very loud squeak."

"A rat?" Tim repeated, unimpressed. "There are a lot of them in these old houses," he said. "Even though you hardly ever see them. They're harmless; you don't have to be afraid."

"*Harmless*?" Victoria repeated in a shrill voice. She gave off an unmistakable odor of human fear; almost panic.

She walked once across the room, then along the walls, staring at the floor and, as far as possible, under the furniture. But to look into the gap under the sofa, she would have had to throw herself down on her stomach. Fortunately she didn't do that.

Thus she didn't see any rodents. And I tried my best to look at her completely uncomprehendingly, and at the same time wagging my tail in a calm, relaxed way. That was my usual demeanor when I wanted to signal to her that "Everything's okay, human."

At the same time, however, I was in the greatest turmoil. Rémy's words were echoing in my head—*we've got her!*

So maybe I was wagging my tail quite tranquilly, but at the same time I was panting so excitedly that poor Victoria must have thought her dog was having a heart attack ... possibly because he was also afraid of rats.

29

Victoria walked to her laptop, lifted it back up onto her thighs, and smiled at Tim with an effort.

"Maybe I just imagined that rat squeal," she said, "although..."

She shook her head. Then she said goodbye to Tim and did me the favor of leaving the room to go to the kitchen. Humans like to reach for food or drink when they are agitated.

I took the opportunity to look under the sofa, where Rémy now sat silent and motionless.

"You found her?" I asked hopefully. "Pearl?"

"We did!" Rémy announced proudly, but at least now he was quiet enough that he could not be heard all the way to the kitchen. My excited yelping and barking would have drowned him out anyway.

"Where?" I exclaimed. "Where is she? Is she ... okay?"

"She's alive," Rémy confirmed. "She's not hurt, I don't think. But she's trapped; we can't free her. We're not strong enough to do that."

"Where?" I repeated. I had no lack of strength. I would get my midget free, no matter what had been done to her!

"Over at the Bruckhausens'—under the roof. My friends are with her."

Under the roof ... that was one place where I hadn't

ventured in my search for Pearl.

Like an echo of my thoughts, Rémy said, "Took us a while to find her there. The attic is not an interesting place to us; there's nothing edible there, just old junk. It's cold in winter, hot in summer..."

"Yes, yes all right," I cried. "Are you coming?" I asked then. I had to leave immediately.

"I'll stay with Pop for a bit, if you don't mind," Rémy said, glancing at his father, who was stretching sleepily.

"Wassup?" Three-tooth muttered.

I sprinted to the kitchen and barked so loudly at Victoria that she almost dropped the glass of water she was sipping.

I nudged her, perhaps a little too vigorously, because a startled "Ouch!" escaped her, then I ran into the hall, positioned myself in front of the door, and barked again like a wild thing.

"You want to go for a walk?" said Victoria. "Okay ... I think I could use some fresh air, too, if I'm already hallucinating rat squeals."

She put the leash on me, then paused for a moment. "Oh God, Athos, I hope I actually imagined it. Do you really think there are rats in our house?"

"Certainly not," I panted impatiently—like a true hypocrite.

"You would be able to track rats, wouldn't you, Athos? And kill them? Or at least chase them away."

I objected that hunting rats was more of a cat thing, apart from the fact that Three-tooth was not much smaller than our little Pearl and would certainly not have made easy prey for her.

Of course, Victoria did not understand a word as usual.

I jumped up and down impatiently in front of the door. "Can we leave now, instead of philosophizing about rats?" I urged.

Finally she opened the front door, and I pulled her at breakneck speed first out onto the street and then across to the Bruckhausens' mansion. Twice I almost tore her off her feet because I had set too ambitious a pace.

Arriving at the main door of the mansion, I positioned myself on the stairs and intoned a wild howl.

Victoria had the presence of mind to understand that I wanted to enter. "What is it, Athos?" she asked, at the same time pressing the bell button. "What are we doing here?"

Erwin opened the door for us shortly thereafter. I could see Victoria struggling sheepishly for words, to give him a reason for our visit, but I held back no longer. I tore myself away from her—fortunately without bringing her down—and rushed up the big staircase that started in the hall. The attic ... how was I to get there?

I heard Erwin shouting angrily after me, but I ignored the old grouch.

Victoria also passed him and came hurrying up the stairs behind me. I heard her footsteps, and she was also calling for me.

Having reached the top of the stairs, I looked around. As on the other floors, there were several corridors leading in different directions. I had already been up here, but I couldn't remember where the stairs to the attic were to be found. But that's what paws were for, after all.

I ran off into the first of the corridors, but soon came to a dead end. So I tried the next one.

In the third corridor I finally found it: a door that was made of metal and fortunately had a conventional handle. It took me four attempts to get it open in my anxious state.

Behind the door I discovered a somewhat dusty stone staircase that led upstairs, and which smelled a bit stale. I was in the right place here!

I barked while rushing up the stairs so that Victoria could find me. It might attract Erwin, too, but he would not dare to attack me again in her presence.

The attic was just as large and spacious as the floors below. Fortunately there were no walls here, however, just a few brick pillars on which the roof beams rested. I called for Pearl, called for the rats—and listened.

I could hear nothing of Pearl. But within seconds I perceived the patter of tiny paws, and then the first rat appeared in front of me. He kept a respectful distance from me, but called out, "This way, dog. The cat's back there."

I followed the rodent, my heart beating so hard that I could hardly breathe. He led me through a maze of discarded furniture, old boxes and crates, almost to the other end of the attic. There was dust everywhere, tickling my nose, but I didn't let that stop me. And finally I could hear her with my own ears: Pearl! A soft meowing, which became louder the further I followed the rat.

The rodent finally came to a stop in front of a large, heavy wooden chest. "She's in there," he said. "But we can't get the lid off. Can you?"

He gave me an awed look, as if he thought I was capable of the greatest of heroic deeds.

I ran toward the chest, barking like a maniac. "Pearl? Are you all right?"

"Yes, yes!" came back to me. The wood of the crate muffled her voice so much that her pitiful mewing sounded only like a distant echo. "Get me out of here, Athos!"

"Sure! Right away!"

I tried to push the lid open with my muzzle, but it didn't move an inch.

There was a handle on top of the chest, but it was so small that only human fingers could get under it and use it to lift the lid. To grab it with a snout or a dog's paw was an impossibility.

What a bummer. Victoria had to help me.

"I'll be right back!" I called out to Pearl. "I'm going to get Victoria!" I tried to get my bearings and find my way back through the maze of furniture and boxes.

The rat, realizing what I was up to, came eagerly to my aid. "This way!" he shouted, already scurrying off.

Once again he ran ahead of me, taking me back to the stairs that led down to the floors below. Out of sheer excitement I'd forgotten that I could just have followed my own track in the opposite direction. But with the rat as a guide it went faster anyway.

When I reached the landing I stopped, barking at the top of my lungs, until finally the metal door opened at the bottom of the stairs, and Victoria emerged.

"Athos! What are you doing? Come down here at once!"

"No! You have to come up here!" I barked at her. I ran back and forth, jumped up and down at the top of the stairs until she finally did as I'd asked. She came rushing up the stairs, trying to grab the leash that was still attached to my collar.

The rat had the presence of mind to seek refuge under the nearest piece of furniture. It was a massive box that looked as if it were a few centuries old. Now I had to find my way back to Pearl on my own—but I had a nose too, after all! And I could even recognize my own paw prints in some places, especially the ones that were the most dusty.

I guided Victoria through the maze. She had to duck a few times, or make herself very slim, and she kept trying to grab me. But I eluded her, barked, and ran on.

Step by step, we approached Pearl. Victoria was cursing and kept asking where the hell I was going, but finally I had reached my destination and we stood in front of the chest where my tiny one was trapped.

I called out to Pearl, prompting her to meow as loudly as she could—and luckily that was enough for our human to hear her as well.

Victoria looked at me in disbelief. Was she afraid of being haunted by another hallucination? Probably.

I barked, nudged the chest with my muzzle, and Pearl also meowed her little heart out—and Victoria finally understood what she had to do. She slid her hand into the handle of the chest—and had no trouble pulling the lid open.

Pearl jumped toward her, landing in her arms.

She meowed angrily, "That little monster did this to me! Marlene. She thought I was her kitten now and hid me here. And unfortunately she was clever enough to open the lid only so far that she could pass me food or water. I had no chance to run away! She told me that I would learn to be good and then I would be allowed to get out of the chest again."

"Be good?" I repeated incredulously.

"Well, I wasn't to run from her." Pearl shook herself, sneezed, and then pressed herself into Victoria's arms, trembling with excitement—or was it anger?

"She was even wearing gloves, the shrewd little beast," she continued. "So I couldn't scratch or bite her!"

Our human burst into tears of relief. "Oh, God, Pearl. You're alive!" She gently cradled the tiny one's body with her hands. "You're not hurt, are you?"

Pearl mewed. "No, I'm okay! But I want revenge on the horrible kid who did this to me!"

30

Of course, Victoria didn't understand Pearl's accusation, but while stroking and caressing the kitten, her brow furrowed. She looked into the chest again, saw food scraps and a small bowl of water ... and a doll blanket embroidered with the image of a princess.

I spied the things at the same time she did—and Victoria drew the right conclusions.

"Someone brought you here," she muttered to herself. "Locked you in this chest..." Presumably the doll's blanket put her on the right track as to who the culprit had to be.

When we descended the attic stairs together, Erwin was waiting for us, red-faced with rage.

"How *dare* you?" he hissed at Victoria. "Just barging into our house like that, with your hideous mutt. I am going to—"

He fell silent when he saw Pearl in Victoria's arms, but didn't miss the opportunity to continue his rant immediately. "An impertinence! I will inform Mr. Bruckhausen—"

"Yes, do that," Victoria cut him off. Her voice had lost its usual warmth and gentleness. She stood up to the old creep with a combative look on her face, staring him down so angrily that he took a step back.

"I want to see Mr. Bruckhausen right away," she

affirmed, "and Amalia, too! Go on, find them both!"

I could not believe my eyes: Erwin letting himself be ordered around as if Victoria were his employer. He pulled out his cell phone, called Balduin Bruckhausen, and then without further objection led us to the patriarch's study, which was on the first floor. On the way he made another call, trying to reach Amalia, who only picked up after half an eternity.

"Would she please join her father in his study," Victoria said, and Erwin passed the words on to Amalia.

"And ask her to bring Marlene along, too." My human still sounded furious, and finally stormed past Erwin through the door of Balduin's study.

The patriarch looked completely caught off guard, and Victoria immediately threw a rather chaotic version of events at him. "My kitten ... held captive in your attic. In a chest! She could have suffocated! I'm sure your granddaughter Marlene was behind it. She probably wanted my cat for herself. The child needs urgent psychological care. She may still be very small, but this is a serious criminal act. What's next, I ask you? Will she kidnap people once she is older? Just take what she wants? You should seriously—"

Her torrent of words was interrupted by Amalia and Marlene, who entered the study. When the little girl saw Pearl sitting in Victoria's arms, she burst into tears.

That dampened Victoria's anger a little. I could tell she felt sympathy for the little kidnapper. Amalia, who had no idea what it was all about, looked at Victoria and the midget in confusion while at the same time immediately setting about drying Marlene's tears.

To cut a long story short: Marlene made a full confession. She was so fond of Pearl, she said, that she desperately wanted the kitten for herself. "And I would have taken great care of her," she affirmed, sniffling.

Balduin gave the little girl quite a brutal roasting. Amalia tried a few times to take her daughter's side, but she could not prevail against her father.

Finally Balduin growled, "Get out of my sight, both of you! We'll talk later."

Amalia and Marlene absconded, while Balduin took a deep breath, wiping a few drops of sweat from his forehead.

Then he said to Victoria, "Please, take a seat."

She hesitated. By now, her anger was probably half gone and she wanted nothing more than to return home with Pearl and me. Nevertheless, she complied with the patriarch's request. He was not a man to be contradicted so easily.

He rang for Erwin, told him to bring coffee and cookies, and then apologized to Victoria profusely and with a very embarrassed expression for his granddaughter's "improper behavior."

"It's all right," Victoria said when he had finished. "She's just a kid. We've all done every kind of stupid thing imaginable at that age. But I'd still recommend having her cared for by a child psychologist so she learns to accept boundaries..."

"Yes, thank you for your advice, Dr. Adler," Balduin said stiffly.

Erwin returned soon after, serving the two-leggeds the prescribed coffee and some chocolate cookies.

"Bring something from the kitchen for the two animals, too, Erwin," Balduin ordered. He turned his head, looked down at me, then at the kitten now sitting on Victoria's lap. "These two really deserve some compensation—or a reward, as far as the dog is concerned. How on earth did he manage to find Pearl up in the attic?" He directed the last question back to Victoria.

"I wonder about that, too," she murmured.

In view of this new command, Erwin made a face as if he would have liked to wring Pearl's and my necks, but then murmured, "Yes, Mr. Bruckhausen," and left the room.

"I wouldn't eat anything he serves us," I murmured to Pearl. "Let's get out of here as fast as we can and back home. I've had enough of these maniacs!"

"No, wait," Pearl said.

She hopped off Victoria's lap and joined me. "You don't know it yet, but I have new clues in this murder case! I was managing to spy quite successfully before that little monster got her hands on me and locked me in that ghastly chest."

"Murder case?" I echoed. "Leon is supposed to be the killer. And then he took his own life."

I gave Pearl a brief summary of everything that had happened in her absence. It was quite a lot … you would have thought we'd strayed into one of those insane action movies that the two-leggeds love to watch.

I mentioned that Tim had been attacked and almost

killed, and that Victoria did not believe in the suicide of Leon. I didn't tell her about my own near-death experience in the lake, though, and also concealed that a rat was currently living with us. I probably would have to break that to Pearl gently. On the other hand, the thought ran through my head, she owed her life—or at least her rescue—to the rats.

"And what do you believe?" the midget said, snapping me out of my thoughts. "That Leon is guilty?"

"Um ... I really don't know what to think anymore. Presumably Leon is innocent, but who does that leave who could have murdered him and the others?"

"I don't think Leon is entirely innocent," Pearl said, to my astonishment. "I was able to overhear a conversation that night, before Marlene put me in that chest, you know. So my heroic efforts, followed by the ordeal of my captivity, were not in vain. Secret Agent 008 on a successful mission!"

She puffed herself up and looked at me as if she had just saved the nation. Oh, what am I saying—the whole planet!

"Go ahead and tell me," I prompted her.

She didn't have to be told twice.

"Well," she began in her best conspiratorial tone, "I ducked out of Marlene's room right after she went to bed. I roamed around the house and finally I heard voices. They were very soft, but you know how fantastic my hearing is."

"Oh, yes," I said dutifully.

Pearl purred with satisfaction. "There were two men

talking, right here in this room: in Balduin's study. The door was closed, and just look at it—it's very thick and even padded on the inside. No two-legged would be able to hear through it. But I positioned myself outside and listened. As I said, my hearing..."

"...is really incredible. The very best!"

Pearl eyed me suspiciously. "Are you making fun of me?"

"Meee? I would never dare to do that!"

Oh, it was so wonderful to have my midget back! I would have loved to give her a really wet kiss right on her adorably snub nose. But I controlled myself.

"Who were the men you overheard?" I asked instead.

"Balduin and Leon! I could clearly recognize their voices, and the two of them were arguing. Leon said to Balduin, 'You promised to make me your successor!' He sounded quite angry."

"Successor?" I repeated, confused.

"The old man replied: 'I brought you into the family, despite your very humble roots! Have you already forgotten that? I introduced you to the world of high finance, showed you how to successfully manage large capital funds. How to preserve and to multiply them. And you could have had Sabrina—all you had to do was be patient, you damned hothead! We couldn't pass up such a lucrative groom as Adrian. Don't you see? I know what I'm doing; I've been successful with my marriage policy for decades!'"

I couldn't make head or tail of Pearl's words.

She went on, "Leon then yelled, 'Marriage policy? You

must mean murder policy!' And Balduin snapped back, 'You of all people dare to say that? You who shot Adrian in cold blood on the open street!'"

We were interrupted because Erwin returned to the room, bringing two porcelain bowls containing what appeared to be roasted pieces of beef. Victoria took the bowls, thanked him and put them on the floor in front us. Erwin left without another word.

Neither Pearl nor I touched the food.

Victoria shrugged sheepishly, and said to Balduin, "Apparently they are much too excited to eat," then continued her conversation with him.

I hadn't heard what the two of them were talking about; I was far too captivated by Pearl's report. In any case, Victoria's tone sounded quite friendly again.

"Go on," I urged Pearl breathlessly.

"I couldn't overhear much more," she had to admit. "Leon still said to Balduin: 'Well, now we're partners anyway, old man, whether you like it or not. Why don't you turn me in for Adrian's death? But then you'll go down with me, I swear! And if you get in my way again with Sabrina—'" Pearl ended abruptly.

"That's it?" I exclaimed. "That's all you could hear?"

"Yeah, cause at that moment Marlene kidnapped me! I was so focused on the conversation that I didn't hear her coming. She must have woken up, realized I was no longer in her room, and then probably came looking for me. She grabbed me, wrapped me in a towel so I couldn't scratch or bite her ... and then locked me up in that vile chest!"

I growled to express my sympathy to Pearl.

Balduin suddenly gave a laugh, pointed at me with a sweeping gesture of his hand, and said to Victoria, "Your animals are quite chatty, it seems. You'd almost think they were talking to each other, just as we do."

"My thoughts exactly," Victoria replied with a tender sideways glance at us.

"Humans," Pearl groaned. "As clueless as ever!"

"True ... but what does it all mean now? This argument between Leon and Balduin?"

"I don't know, exactly," Pearl admitted. "But it looks like they're both criminals. Leon definitely killed Adrian."

"But Leon is dead now, too," I pointed out.

"Hmm," Pearl grumbled. "That's bad."

"Did Marlene get any of that argument, too?" I asked. "When she chased you and then kidnapped you outside the study door?"

"I don't think so. She only showed up after a while, and then she grabbed me and ran off with me right away. Besides, she couldn't have heard anything through the door. You have to admit she's still very small. And stupid! No, I don't think she gave a damn about the conversation."

"Crap. That means we don't have a human witness to what you heard. Not even the little monster."

"We need to cross-examine Balduin!" said Pearl. "Find out what he knows. Corner him..." She sounded more like a secret agent than ever.

"Good plan," I agreed with her. "Victoria needs to grill

him about the murders. Only how can we put her on the case?"

31

Our human rose just at that moment, and was about to say goodbye to Balduin. Quick action was required.

"Victoria knows we're clever sleuths by now," I said to Pearl. "She's followed me without objection these past few days, whenever I've tried to lead her somewhere. Well, maybe not completely without objection ... but in the end she always has. Even today she followed me first here to the mansion and then up to you in the attic. And she's already spoken to Tim about the fact that Leon's suicide seems strange to her."

"Maybe we can make her understand that Balduin is a suspect," Pearl said. "That she should grill him!"

"But might that not be dangerous for her?" I asked. "If the old man really is a murderer..."

"Just look at him," Pearl replied grandiosely. "He's an old man; you and I can handle him together. He can't do anything to Victoria."

"Okay. And *how* to sic her on him?" I asked her further.

Victoria was just walking up to Balduin, wanting to shake his hand in farewell. He remained sitting like a king on his office chair behind the desk.

"We growl at him," Pearl suggested. "Then hopefully she'll realize there's something wrong with him, and start asking some critical questions. Do you think she'll do that?"

"We'll never know unless we try!"

"Let's go!" Pearl said. Then she ran up to Balduin's desk and intoned a growl that she must have thought was menacing: the roar of a royal tiger. To my ears it sounded more like a somewhat ill-tempered purr. But fortunately I was there to back her up!

I also ran towards Balduin, pulled my lips back and bared my teeth. *My* growl sounded like that of a mighty alpha wolf!

Balduin raised his eyebrows in fright and pressed himself against the back of his chair. "What's wrong with your pets all of a sudden?" he called out to Victoria.

"Come on you two, let's go!" Victoria told us. She looked most surprised at our behavior, but at the same time she turned to the door, probably hoping that we would follow her.

But we didn't have the slightest intention of doing so. Instead we circled the old man's desk together, Pearl from the right, me from the left.

Only when we were so close to him that I could have given him a wet ear kiss did we stop. Pearl purred—pardon, hissed wildly—at him, and the patriarch was not to receive a lick from me either. Instead, I showed him my teeth and growled threateningly again.

He pressed himself even more firmly against the back of the chair, trying above all to gain some distance from me, but at the same time adopting an imperious tone. "Dr. Adler, do something!"

Victoria looked perplexed, then embarrassed. She

opened her lips, presumably to reprimand us once more. I expected to hear a "Behave yourselves, you two!"—but things played out differently.

She closed her mouth, staring first at Pearl, then at me. I growled a little louder and demonstratively put my paw on the back of the old man's chair. I really couldn't get more explicit than that. And finally Victoria seemed to understand.

"Athos and Pearl are apparently angry with you," she said to Balduin. "And it seems to me that they're both trying to tell me something—maybe that we're not done here? With you?"

"What is this *nonsense*?" protested Balduin, but Victoria took no notice.

Instead, she returned to her chair in front of the desk and took her seat again. Pearl and I fell silent, but continued to flank the old man. He should not get any stupid ideas and try to approach Victoria in any way.

I panted at our human, encouraging her. "You're doing the right thing! Go ahead, cross-examine him. He knows a lot more than you think!"

To my great astonishment, she actually seemed to grasp what I was trying to tell her for once.

She crossed her arms in front of her chest and sought Balduin's gaze. "I actually have some unanswered questions about the murders," she began. "Perhaps we should go over the events again. A lot of what happened seems very strange to me, especially the police's recent conclusions. I'm not a criminal investigator, but the human psyche is my area of work. And that Leon should be guilty of all the murders ... that seems to me highly implausible."

She repeated those concerns she had already expressed to Tim in the video call: she explained to Balduin that she did not think the extended jealousy drama, which was to have included Tim and Sinclair in addition to Adrian, to be conceivable. And that she did not believe in Leon's suicide, either.

"I think Sinclair McAllister lost his life because he found, or rather stole, a notebook of my late father's," she continued. "And I was told that he also died under strange circumstances."

She seemed changed, no longer the empathetic psychotherapist I knew, but almost a prosecutor, the kind you see in TV crime shows. Not tough so much as determined to bring the truth to light.

She leaned forward in her chair, staring intently at Balduin. "Speaking of my father's death, you and Leon were with him on the lake the day that he fell into the water, weren't you? And there was no bad weather, no storm, no high waves—that makes me wonder how that accident could have happened in the first place, and whether my father really suffered a heart attack afterwards."

"Are you out of your mind?" Balduin snapped. He would have liked to jump up and put an end to the conversation, but at his first movement I made it clear to him that it was not a good idea.

"Sit, human!" Pearl commanded him with her superbly dangerous snarl.

Balduin had no choice but to obey. He stayed where he was, and Victoria continued to speak, unperturbed. She really got going now, talking faster, more confidently, and glaring wildly at the patriarch as she did so.

"You know more than you care to admit!" she threw at him. "A lot more. And you call the shots in this house. You pull the strings ... the only question is to what extent."

"Now listen, my dear Dr. Adler!" Balduin tried again to defend himself.

"No, you listen to me for once! You may be used to always getting your way in this house. Sabrina listened to you about her marriage—"

"So what?" Balduin, by now red with anger, cut her off. "I told her that Adrian was the more suitable fellow, more stable and reliable than Leon, although I liked him too. It was for Sabrina's own good!"

Victoria tried to object, but the old man wouldn't let her get a word in edgewise. He couldn't stand up, I knew how to prevent that, but he dared to lean forward and bang his fist on the desk top at least.

"My family affairs are none of your business," he cried. "I must say, I find your behavior most disconcerting! Until now I have held you in high esteem, and as you know your father was one of my best friends. But now I've had enough! Get a grip on your animals and get out of my house right now!"

I briefly had the impression that Victoria was letting herself be intimidated. She narrowed her eyes and seemed to be searching for the right words. But to my great delight she did not give up. Instead of taking her leave, she pestered the patriarch with a new question.

"Speaking of marriage plans," she said, "you also interfered with Amalia's, but not for the better. You forbade her the doctor ... and I wonder why. Is his income too modest? Somehow it's always about money with you, isn't it? And Adrian was probably a hundred times richer than Leon."

"I was only concerned about the welfare of my girls." The old man was becoming incensed, but Victoria didn't seem to hear him at all. Her voice now gained strength and speed again.

She continued as if talking to herself: "Yes, it was about the money. Your family treasure that my father was looking for on your behalf ... you claimed to me that it had played no role in your family fortunes, but Sabrina told me something completely different. She claimed that your family was plagued by great financial worries after Artur passed away, because he never revealed the treasure's hiding place. It was only when you grew up and became the new head of the family that the tide turned. Then things looked brighter again financially ... but for no apparent reason, it seems to me. So you lied to me about that chapter of your family history. Perhaps it was not merely out of false pride, as I first believed?"

"Hey, she's doing really well, don't you think?" I said to Pearl. I panted encouragingly to Victoria to continue. She didn't need to be told twice.

"According to my father's documents, he was not only

immersing himself in the treasure hunt," she addressed Balduin again, "but in the process also intensively studying the history of your family. And in doing so, he came across certain deaths that seemed strange to him—Sabrina's father, Amalia's husband—and perhaps other deaths in the more distant past? In any case, the murders of the last few days are apparently not a new event, nor an isolated case in your family history. I wonder when it started, the dying ... perhaps since *you* came to power?"

Balduin laughed harshly. Then he deliberately tapped his index finger against his temple. "You advised me earlier that I should send Marlene to a psychotherapist," he hissed, "but it seems to me that you would need such mental help much more yourself."

Victoria grimaced. This statement probably affected her professional honor, but fortunately did not throw her completely off track.

"I was only able to review some of my father's notes," she continued. "Others—the really explosive ones?— were probably contained in the notebook Sinclair McAllister stole. Did he come to you with it—to blackmail you? The night he died, he left his hotel armed— and never returned. Did you silence him? Just as you silenced my father when he found out about your dirty little secret?"

Victoria was speaking faster and faster, talking herself increasingly into a frenzy and expressing thoughts that seemed all too coherent to me.

Balduin was still playing the angry patriarch, but I

could smell that he was feeling increasingly cornered. What Victoria was throwing at him could not be too far from the truth.

"You murdered Sinclair," Victoria accused the old man, "knocked him down and threw him in the lake—and when his death didn't pass for suicide, you quickly had a scapegoat ready. The gardener with a criminal record; he was perfect for the role, wasn't he? And you did a great job falsifying the evidence."

Balduin's body tensed. A throbbing vein of anger appeared on his forehead. And then he did something that I had not foreseen.

His right hand snapped forward, ripped open the large desk drawer that was directly in front of him—and pulled out a pistol.

I heard Pearl let out a startled squeak and realized to my horror that Balduin was pointing the gun at Victoria. I was halfway to sinking my teeth into his arm, but just managed to stop myself. If I did that, I would undoubtedly succeed in breaking his bones, but he might still be able to pull the trigger ... and as close as Victoria was to him, he couldn't possibly miss.

I froze in place.

Balduin let out a hideous laugh as he set his sights on my human.

"That's really enough, my dear," he said in an icy tone, seemingly completely calm. "You may think you're clever, but that was also your old man's undoing, as you so eloquently pointed out just now. It will probably be difficult to explain your death, but I'll think of something. I've always managed to come up with a suitable idea. And I certainly won't let you ruin everything for me, after all the sacrifices I've made."

"*Sacrifices*?" Victoria exclaimed. "You mean murders!"

I could tell she was scared, but she tried to stand her ground despite everything. She did not retreat, nor did she resort to begging for her life. My brave human!

The old man brooded, staring at her for a moment, then suddenly a grin flitted across his grizzled features.

"Ha, I got it!" he announced triumphantly. "Your mutt went crazy and tried to attack me. I reached for the pistol in my desk drawer to fight back. An overreaction, I might have to be blamed for that, but after all, your beast is no lap dog. You wanted to intervene, to protect him ... and unfortunately the bullet hit you. A tragic accident—"

"Take cover," I murmured to Pearl, "I'll pounce on him!"

"Don't!" she hissed. "He'll hit Victoria! Or you!"

I hesitated, unsure...

At that moment, the door of the study flew open. Amalia came rushing in, her smallest child in her arms, leading Marlene by the other hand.

"Ah, Victoria," she began, "you're still here, how nice! Marlene wanted to apologize to you again—about the, um, kidnapping of your kitten. She drew a picture, with you, Athos and Pearl—"

She fell silent abruptly as her brain processed what she

was seeing before her. Her father holding a pistol in his hand—which was pointed right at Victoria. "B-but..." she stammered.

Little Marlene, who probably didn't know what a gun was, detached herself from her mother's hand and ran up to Victoria, stopping right in front of her and holding out the sheet of paper with the painted picture.

"I'm really sorry," she mumbled. Unwittingly she'd walked right into her grandfather's line of fire.

At that moment, I could have hugged the little monster. She'd saved all our lives.

Balduin lowered the hand with the gun ... and began to sob.

"I did it for all of you!" he cried, staring at Amalia. "That you should never suffer any hardship—to live in abundance, in dignity and prestige, even if one day I shall be no more..."

32

Victoria was waiting in the car just outside the hospital's main entrance when Tim appeared. He was being pushed out of the building in a wheelchair by an orderly, but straightened up on a pair of crutches as Victoria ran to meet him.

Pearl and I were also part of the reception committee, of course. Victoria threw herself at Tim a little too impetuously, making the poor man almost lose his balance. She apologized, looking sheepish, and helped him hop on his crutches to her car.

"Whew, this hobbling is really working on my arm muscles!" he complained jokingly. "By the time they get my cast off and I'm allowed to put weight on my foot again, I'll have upper arms like a hulk. I hope you're into strong men?" he teased Victoria.

"Oh, yes," she replied with a laugh, pulling him into her arms again.

At home on the sofa, she told him all about the events that had really come to a head only in the last few days. She had already filled him in on a few details by video phone, but it seemed to do her good to get everything off her chest once again in person.

Pearl settled on Tim's belly as he stretched out on the

sofa, which meant "Welcome to our home," while I confined myself to getting comfortable on the rug next to the sofa table and listening to Victoria's report. Pearl and I found more than one honorable mention in it.

After our dramatic showdown in the study, Balduin Bruckhausen had been arrested by the police, and had offered no resistance. When they'd taken him away, in front of his closest family members, he had been just a heap of misery—a broken old man who was weeping bitterly.

The confession that he had subsequently made was reproduced in full by Inspector Zimmermann to the Bruckhausen family and also to Victoria.

In the financial hardship following the death of Artur, when the young Balduin became head of the family, he had taken his cue from the marriage policy of the Habsburgs, as he put it. For centuries the former Austrian imperial family had known how to expand the borders of their empire and increase their wealth through clever marriage alliances.

Earning money through work was in Balduin's eyes beneath the dignity of a respectable family that counted itself among the elite, so he relied on wealthy spouses to fill the coffers of the Bruckhausens and provide them with a lifestyle 'befitting their station.'

In order to be able to marry rich himself, Balduin had murdered his first wife, who had no assets worth mentioning. She had been sickly anyway, so he'd thought, and he had acted only for the good of the family. The Bruckhausens were to be restored to their former glory and prestige, and that was the motto to which he'd remained true for the next several decades.

So everything had begun with the murder of his own wife. She had been Balduin's first victim—but by no means his last. He'd relied on great fertility, on numerous offspring, even if he himself had only had three children. He'd known how to marry them off in a way that promised a profit. He'd interfered as a matter of course in their marriage plans, and later in those of his grandchildren, in order to bring wealthy men and women into the family. If these spouses were willing to submit to his will and leave their capital to his management, they were allowed to live on. As, for example, Edith had done, having brought a considerable fortune into her marriage with Maxim.

On the other hand, anyone who'd rebelled against Balduin's rule or merely tried to defy him had suffered a tragic accident or died of a mysterious illness, with their inheritance falling to the spouse's family—that is, the Bruckhausens. Children widowed in this way had been remarried wherever possible, and of course in such cases again only rich partners were eligible. Simple country doctors of the caliber of Dr. Guido Rauch were undesirable.

My professor had actually set off in search of the Bruckhausens' treasure just for fun, but in the process had come across these accumulated strange deaths, and finally Balduin's secret. He couldn't have known, however, that he was risking his life on that boat trip that he'd taken with Balduin on the lake. After all, Leon had been there, too, and my poor professor had had no idea that Balduin had made Sabrina's young suitor his sidekick. More than that, the aging mass murderer had chosen Leon as his successor.

And so my poor professor had been drowned by them in the lake. They'd brought him—when he was long dead—back to the mansion, where they pretended that he had merely suffered an accident and lost consciousness. They'd put him in a guest room and had not allowed anyone to see him, even though they'd ordered food and drink from the staff for their poor friend. They'd done the latter only to conceal the fact that the professor was already dead. Then, during the night, he'd allegedly suffered a heart attack. That, in turn, was nothing particularly unusual for an old man.

The next morning, when the dead man was discovered, only the village doctor had been called. He had not carried out a meticulous examination to determine the exact time and actual cause of death, but had dutifully signed the death certificate. After all, he hadn't wanted to offend his future father-in-law. At the time Dr. Guido Rauch had still been hoping to be allowed to marry Amalia.

In the case of a death on the lake, as a direct result of a boating accident—unlike a heart attack, which had apparently occurred later—at least the local police would have had to be called in. And they might have insisted on investigating the death more closely. A boating accident in fair weather was quite unusual after all....

"What do you mean Balduin wanted to make Leon his

successor?" Tim interrupted Victoria's account. He apparently didn't know anything about that yet.

"Leon was anything but rich, right?" he said. "So he didn't fit in at all with Balduin's marriage policy. What an expression to use to describe a decades-long series of murders!" Tim shook his head.

"Leon was really not rich," Victoria said, "but still, he was very ambitious and also clever. Not to mention ruthless. He wanted to make it to the top of the social ladder and was willing to literally walk over dead bodies to do so. Although he seemed to really love Sabrina; that was important to Balduin, because for all his murderous machinations the old man was always concerned about the welfare of his family ... or at least he put them in second place, after the increase of his fortune. Only outsiders were murdered to inherit their money; none of the family members was ever harmed in any way. But Balduin was getting old, his days were numbered, and among his own descendants there was no man suitable to be the all-controlling patriarch who would secure the future of the family."

"No potential murderer, you mean to say," Tim objected.

"That's one way to put it, yes. And that's why Leon came along just in time. Balduin initiated him into his marriage policy and tried to teach him the fine art of investing money as well, so that he could continue the family's financial business. As far as the stock exchange goes, Balduin is apparently extremely talented—not merely at murder.

"But then a second admirer of Sabrina suddenly appeared: Adrian Seeberg. And he was so rich that Balduin could not resist.

"So the patriarch made a plan, which went like this: Adrian would marry Sabrina first, and then, shortly after the marriage, suffer a fatal accident. Sabrina would inherit his fortune and be only too happy to leave her capital to her father to manage and increase. After all, the family members, including Sabrina, were used to living a life of idleness. Leon was supposed to win back Sabrina's heart after Adrian's death and then be her second husband, eventually becoming the new head of the family after Balduin's death. So all Leon had to do was show a little patience—but he wasn't willing to do that."

I could understand his behavior, in a way. When it comes to love, some humans are not to be trifled with. Leon didn't want to leave the woman he desired to another man, even if it might have been a lucrative business deal. And so he defied Balduin's plans: he killed Adrian.

"With the help of the Bruckhausens' exterior cameras, Leon must have seen you leaving my house that night," Victoria told Tim, "when you were already on the run from the police. He followed you, discovered your hiding place in the old forestry cabin, and since you were already wanted for Sinclair's murder he decided to make you a scapegoat for Adrian's death as well."

"By letting me die miserably in that bear trap," Tim growled. He lowered his eyes, looking down at me. "It's only thanks to Athos that I'm still alive."

I basked in the glow of his approval.

"If you had died in the bear trap," Victoria said, "Leon's plan probably would have worked out. You would have been charged with the two murders and the case would have been closed."

But Balduin had not tolerated Leon's defiance of his will. A successor who disobeyed and shot a rival in the heat of passion was no longer a suitable candidate. Leon went from being the potential future head of the family to being a burden that Balduin had to get rid of. He murdered him by first giving him a sleeping draught and then administering a lethal dose of drugs. And luck seemed to be on Balduin's side one more time: the police believed the suicide theory and would probably have closed the case.

"It's only thanks to you that the old man didn't get away with all his crimes," Tim told Victoria.

"Me? Oh no; it was Athos and Pearl who urged me to go after Balduin. They growled at him like mad and refused to leave the room. I thought they were trying to tell me that Balduin was guilty."

Tim laughed and cuddled Pearl's little head. "You and I are really hopeless fools when it comes to pets, Victoria. We have to be careful not to humanize these two cuties too much. I mean, if we already think they can solve murders, where does that leave us?"

Pearl straightened up and twitched her ears in exasperation. "Oh how I hate being underestimated like this all the time!"

"Ah," I said. "I guess we'll just have to live with it. As

long as the two-leggeds do what we want anyway, there's nothing wrong with that, right?"

"Oh well," the midget said, mollified, and settled back down on Tim's belly.

After Balduin had been arrested, Amalia took over the vacant position of head of the family, to everyone's great surprise. Her first official act was to fire Erwin, which was greeted with great applause by all the family members—and by us!

Secondly, she accepted Dr. Guido Rauch's marriage proposal, and the two started planning their wedding with Father Valentin.

Victoria was in and out of the Bruckhausens' home regularly over the next few weeks. She gave comfort, helping both the young and the elderly to come to terms with the tragic events as best she could. Pearl and I, of course, were in on the action, repeatedly referred to by Victoria as her co-therapists, and bravely sacrificed ourselves to perform various cuddles.

Only Marlene was carefully avoided by us, and for her part she also refrained from coming too close to Pearl again. Every now and then I caught the girl casting a longing glance at the kitten, but that was all. Amalia hinted that she might have a kitten of her own when she was a bit older. One could only hope that she would be more careful with the poor animal by then.

The Bruckhausens prepared themselves for the possibility of having to get by with far less money in the future. Fabius and Sabrina even announced that they would not object to getting a job. But it wasn't to come to that, because luck was with the family.

When Tim was finally able to use both his legs again, he took Victoria and the rest of us to the Bruckhausens' overgrown park—where, after a few detours, he found the statue of the goddess Hathor. And at her feet, buried under her pedestal, we discovered the secret hiding place of Artur Bruckhausen's treasure.

The chest we unearthed with our combined efforts—this time no one complained about my passion for digging!—was full of gold and jewels, more than anyone could have dreamed of.

The Bruckhausens were speechless, and infinitely grateful. Their future was secured for generations, without ever having to resort to Balduin Bruckhausen's marriage policy again.

Amalia proved to be extremely generous. Tim and Victoria each received five percent of the treasure as a finder's fee, and Pearl and I were given a feast prepared especially for us by Sammy, the cook.

I smuggled some of the treats back into our house in my jaws, to the patient who was still living under our sofa. Unlike Tim, Three-tooth didn't have a cast or crutches available to help heal his leg, but he too was slowly able to move his hind paws again—every day a little bit more.

When Victoria wasn't home, the rodent was already bravely walking longer distances up and down our living room. He swayed a bit, and rather reminded us of a sailor, but Pearl and I were confident that he would soon be quite his old rat-self again.

Now that Erwin was gone, Three-tooth could hardly wait to move back into the Bruckhausens' pantry.

"The real land of milk and honey!" he kept repeating, his dark beady eyes gleaming with excitement. "But even if I move out of your house again, we'll still be friends, right?" He added, "I really love having met you guys! Even though the circumstances may have been a little rough."

Rémy, on the other hand, continued to be rebuffed in his quest to obtain an assistant's job in Sammy's kitchen. He would have to rethink his career plans—or, in keeping with the Bruckhausen tradition, devote himself to idleness, as his father had already successfully demonstrated to him. Unfortunately, a happy ending for everyone is only possible on the television screen.

More from Athos and Pearl:

THE WEDNESDAY EVENING CLUB
A Case for the Master Sleuths, Book 3

Psychotherapist Victoria Adler is introduced to a spooky reading circle at her newest client's estate. Every Wednesday evening, the classics and the latest bestsellers of the paranormal genre are read together—but then a guest of the club suddenly dies under the strangest circumstances. One could almost think he'd fallen victim to a deadly spell, just like in the old horror stories.
Athos and Pearl are once again in demand as four-pawed detectives, before another two-legged loses his life....

About the author

Alex Wagner lives with her husband and 'partner in crime' near Vienna, Austria. From her writing chair she has a view of an old ruined castle, which helps her to dream up the most devious murder plots.

Alex writes murder mysteries set in the most beautiful locations in Europe and in popular holiday spots. If you love to read Agatha Christie and other authors from the Golden Age of mystery fiction, you will enjoy her stories.

www.alexwagner.at
www.facebook.com/AlexWagnerMysteryWriter
www.instagram.com/alexwagner_author

Cover design: Estella Vukovic
Editor: Tarryn Thomas

www.alexwagner.at

Printed in Great Britain
by Amazon